D1372803

THE VERITY SCANNER
by Edward McClenathan

Cover art by the Author

For my son,
Todd McClenathan

His wife,
Barbara Arnesen McClenathan

Their daughter,
Elena McClenathan

My enduring gratitude
For making this book possible.

Table of Contents

NOTE ON THE TRANSLATOR

"In proportion as we perceive and embrace the truth
do we become just, heroic, magnanimous, divine."

- William Lloyd Garrison, *Free Speech and Free Inquiry.*

"Truth is a shining goddess, always veiled,
always distant, never wholly approachable,
but worthy of all the devotion of which the
human spirit is capable."

-Bertrand Russell, *Facts and Fiction.*

"Truth will ultimately prevail where
there is pains taken to bring it to light."

- George Washington, *Maxims.*

NOTE ON THE TRANSLATION

This translation proved to be particularly problematic. I had to work many times past exhaustion because of the short time permitted by the deadline. In addition to that, the foreign nature of the story made it difficult to find the appropriate idioms to express the content of the narrative. Conversations were especially difficult. And sometimes the circumstances were so unbearable, it made me uneasy.

I wouldn't have endured the strain of the translation, had I not believed the subject important to place before the public. I am firmly convinced that it is a most significant book, not only because of its source, but also what I learned from it. If a book could ever hope to influence solutions to current problems, this one must.

I think the reader may benefit from it now, but I hope I will be permitted more time to work on the translations.

The Translator

CHAPTER I

The rocket launch was scheduled for the next morning.

Sara rolled over against Kronkite. Their bodies touching felt softly warm. Someone who has lost a life companion especially knows the comfort of such intimacy. Kronkite put his arm around his wife.

Their thoughts were full of the evening's festivities. The bon voyage party left them tired but content.

"I hope we chose well," said Sara.

"Our courageous astronauts, you mean?" said Kronkite. "Yes, it's all so final, isn't it?"

Kronkite and Sara were a devoted husband and wife team. He was a scientist and inventor, she, a psychologist. Her specialty was personality. He was a master of technology. Together, they were more than marital partners. Through the years, they had been a dynamic duo.

"It's out of our hands now. It's all up to weather, rocketry, and that most important factor, luck," said Kronkite, giving Sara an affirming hug. "I can't think of anything else we could have done to make tomorrow's launch successful."

"Are you worried?" Sara asked.

"Worried? Sure, I'm worried. But when that fear gets to me, I say to myself '*You believe in me. So, dig in. Get to work!*' And you know what? That's all I need." He kissed her playfully on the cheek.

Sara smiled to herself and snuggled closer. "I wonder if they are sleeping well?"

"I don't imagine sleep came easy this night, whether ground crew or astronauts."

"There's such a finality to it all, isn't there?" Sara added.

"That's for sure," he nodded in agreement. "They deserve a damned lot of admiration. I'm only sad we'll never know the final outcome."

"Me, too," she agreed. "You've been the inspiration, but they are the future. I just wonder how you'll be remembered. Will it be for the Verity Scanner, or tomorrow's launch?"

"Only time will tell. My reputation is on the line. Of course, we'll never know if this mission will succeed in saving our species far in the future or not."

11

As a young man, Kronkite had invented the Verity Scanner, which completely revolutionized and revitalized the entire social makeup of their world. Because of his invention, it was no longer possible to tell an undetected lie.

The design of the device was ingenious; both simple and complex. No physical attachments to the person being tested were required. Only his auditory and visual presence. The Scanner was effective pointed at the person, or merely pointed at his televised image. It was totally unobtrusive.

While auditing a speaker, the Scanner produced a readout or printout which Kronkite titled the "V.I.P.", an acronym for Verity Indicator Profile. It was a tripartite test of a person's character, his statements, and his veracity. The data (visual and auditory) was transmitted to a mega memory computer which rendered an analysis almost instantaneously.

The first analysis was a test of the person, his life, and character. Each exposure to the Verity Scanner augmented or diminished the person's Reputation File. Vanity, racism, bigotry, credulity, chauvinism, avariciousness. Any negative traits were compiled there. Positive traits such as adherence to facts, reliability, truthfulness, etc. also were recorded.

The second analysis was a test of the speaker's voice (pitch, pace, cadence, breath arrhythmia), tremors, duplicitous smiles, shifty eyes, involuntary facial tics, inappropriate, contrived or exaggerated gestures. Had a liar no negative Reputation File, this probing analysis exposed him anyway.

The third and final analysis was the factual test. Claims made by a speaker had to be substantiated by concrete evidence. All facts were instantly checked by a huge encyclopedic database to be corroborated by the Verity Scanner. It consisted only of verified facts. All irrationality, superstition, unproven theories, and suppositions were expunged from the encyclopedic bank's files. As one wag put it: "Bullshit won't fly anymore."

Kronkite had his own corny joke about his invention. "People will no longer be myth-informed. And I'm not lisping when I say that."

The autumn of its first demonstration, the Verity Scanner became headline news. It held the public's fascination like an earthquake. It was the lead story on all of the networks. Kronkite was an immediate celebrity. Some individuals and groups who had gained power through lies and deception—and there were many— attempted every ploy to suppress its use. But the public clamored for it. And Kronkite could not be bought off.

Three factors disarmed the opponents. First, all past lying malefactors could henceforth reform and be truthful. They had the opportunity for a fresh start. Second, there were no penalties for lying, other than there was no longer any gain or profit to be made from lies. And third, opposing the Verity Scanner was almost an admission of guilt.

12

Finally, since there was no coercion or invasion of privacy with the Scanner, it had the approval of the civil libertarians.

From that autumn on, its development exploded. Demand for the product was tremendous.

Major newscasters and government agencies vied with one another to purchase the first production models. Then the prototypes underwent miniaturization. And mass production lowered the cost to the consumer, so that it became as readily available as a radio, television, or cellphone. Almost every family purchased one. Some owned more than one.

The effect on civilization was startling. Politicians could no longer lie to get into office. Fake news was exposed. Greedy tyrants could no longer fill their pockets at taxpayer's expense, or lead people into disastrous wars. Swindlers and quacks could no longer find followers for their schemes and cults. Salesmen could no longer misrepresent their products. Corrupt financiers could no longer deceive investors. Frauds could no longer make false insurance claims. Insurance adjusters could no longer deny legitimate claims. Regulators and police officers could no longer be negligent, incompetent, or accept bribes. Criminals could no longer deny their guilt. Every sharp and unscrupulous practice was brought under severe scrutiny.

Lies, which for centuries had so misled the public into faction and strife, were finally exposed for all to see. With the Verity Scanner, a new standard of honesty was inaugurated— a new era of truth.

It became starkly apparent to everyone everywhere that a world of lies, myths, and fanaticism, is a world of strife. Once the perpetrators were unmasked by the Verity Scanner, their supporters melted away like the snow in springtime. Prosperity increased as the existence of crime, deceit, and weapons of war decreased. People in great numbers could no longer be mobilized toward ignoble ends. One could no longer fool even the fools. All benefited by increased discernment. The level of education rose as misinformation and indoctrination was dispelled. It was the death knell of hypocrisy and dissimulation. New leaders of vision and merit came to the forefront. With the advent of honest and fair relationships, harmony among people increased.

The Verity Scanner era had such an astounding influence, that the whole world designated historic time as B.K. or A.K— *before* Kronkite or *after* Kronkite.

Not satisfied with all his hard-earned accolades, Kronkite was about to put his august reputation on the line once more. This time to send four specially selected explorers out into space to seek other worlds. A safeguard to save humanity in case of a world catastrophe, such as a comet collision or a climatic disaster. The project was a dream shared by Sara and Kronkite, and the world in general.

Meeting years before at university, the two had been drawn to each other, and they had married soon after. As a young psychologist, Sara had developed the personality profile test called "CHARM QUOTA". It was her test that was used to select the four astronauts from the applicants. From the start, Sara and Kronkite were an extraordinary team.

Sara cuddled closer to Kronkite. "If Atom, Evelyn, Orwell, and Darla are awake yet, I wonder what they are thinking about. This has to be the most suspenseful night of their lives."

"Suspenseful or agonizing," said Kronkite. "Think of having your companionship reduced to three people for who knows how long."

"Certainly, the quarantine period demonstrated the rapport they have with one another."

"Yes, both factors are important, obviously," he continued. "The introduction of disease into the spaceship would doom the mission from the start. But the unknown over which we have no control is... will they remain companionable over such an extended period of time? And especially in such cramped quarters."

"My hope is that they will be as happy as we have been in our nearly forty-eight years of marriage," said Sara.

"Ah, yes, I hope so too, darling," he agreed. "But they are so young, so young. Their adult lives are just beginning. What sets my mind most at ease is that I have great confidence in your personality profile of them"

"I hope we made a wise choice in choosing Atom over Jordon," Sara said.

"Why?" asked Kronkite. "You don't have any doubt at this point, do you?"

"Jordon was stronger physically," said Sara.

"That won't make much difference in weightlessness," Kronkite chuckled. Then he added parenthetically, "At least they're weightless until centrifugal gravity kicks in. Atom's test clearly showed superior leadership potential. Besides, I feel that Atom shared our values and will carry on our life's work."

Sara agreed. "Yes, Atom has rare qualities. Orphaned at an early age, his parents dedicated scientists. And what a unique name for this assignment— A-T-O-M. It's almost as if his parents had destined him for it."

"Let's hope he develops the necessary qualities for the job," Kronkite mused. "The journey is not going to be easy, not for any of them."

"He and Evelyn seem well suited to each other," offered Sara.

"Yes, they are a nice couple," he agreed, "as are Orwell and Darla, for that matter. Nonetheless, it will have to be a team effort to succeed, or I fear it'll seem like a prison sentence. I sometimes worry whether I'm doing right by them. Have I become overly obsessed by the project?"

"Leave the psychoanalyses to me, dear. That's my specialty," Sara laughed. "Don't you dare intrude on my territory; my department."

"Believe me, I wouldn't think of it," smiled Kronkite.

"You know, dear," reflected Sara, "Atom looks up to you as a father—perhaps as the father he never knew."

"Yes, Sara, and I believe Orwell looks up to Atom as a big brother. In many ways, Atom, Orwell, Evelyn, and Darla are like our children, carrying on the work we began. I wish there was room on the 'Starfarer' for us, or that we were in their shoes, just starting our lives. But there wouldn't be time for us to reach the 'promised land' ... or should I say land-*ing*? Think of it. They are the ultimate in explorers with little or no probability of returning to their home planet."

"Fantastic, isn't it?" Sara added. "But who knows, maybe in some distant time their offspring will make a return trip. It's exciting to think about it. They'll be pioneers in the wilderness of space."

"That's for sure," he agreed. "However, we'd better get some sleep. There's a lot to do tomorrow."

They kissed goodnight. "Are you going to miss the project terribly once it's over?" Sara asked.

"No, I think we'll treat ourselves to a much-deserved vacation and a little..." he gently laughed, "...a little unbridled lust."

"Oh," mused Sara, "is that a promise?"

Kronkite nodded. "That's a promise, darling."

CHAPTER II

Within a decade, a burst of creative energy circled the globe. Time and energy formerly wasted on debilitating fear and suspicion which accompany lies and deception, were channeled instead toward positive and worthy goals. Capital dried up for parasitic leaders, groups, and organizations, and became available for productive and worthwhile ends. With the Verity Scanner, people of modest intelligence and rationality had a defense against demagoguery.

Relationships between family members, friends, and even strangers, improved. People were able to understand others and themselves better. A new honesty came into dealings between workers and managers. Entrepreneurs who espoused genuine values were greeted with enthusiastic support.

Curiosity and creativity became highly valued attributes. The Verity Scanner ushered in a golden age.

The Starfarer Space Project was an outgrowth of the new era. The towering rocket, like a skyscraper silhouetted against a dawn-streaked sky, symbolized the new creativity and curiosity.

It was a gigantic enterprise; a collaborative effort funded and supported by millions and millions of people. There had been a tremendous outpouring of assistance and contributions from scientific and academic communities. Industries were for it because it created employment. The goal— space; the ultimate exploration. And who was most trusted to supervise the new project? Who better than the renowned inventor of the Verity Scanner, Kronkite, benefactor of all. A person not mired in the past, but dedicated to progress and the future.

Kronkite was, however, too old to accompany the mission. Therefore, four young volunteer astronauts were selected. All of them under twenty-one.

At dawn, the control headquarters was already a beehive of activity when Kronkite arrived. The workers intently read gauges, checked systems, and scanned weather forecasts on radar. Diodes flashed measuring outputs in colorful arrays. Technicians examined seeming minutia under extreme magnification. Kronkite always insisted: "Faulty factual details lead to faulty conclusions, which consequently, lead to faulty results." With the spaceship, it could mean fatal results. As he put it, "Good enough is <u>not</u> good enough."

With the Verity Scanner, it was no longer possible to duck responsibility through equivocation. But it was still possible to err because of the ancient enemies: negligence, incompetence, or the failure to ask and demand accurate answers to all questions. It opened minds that had been closed for ages. All beliefs were subject to factual evidence.

The crew prepared to perform the extensive countdown checklist as Kronkite, standing by the glass enclosure, awaited the astronauts. He felt a pang in his heart. He had grown to love the four young people as children whom he'd never had. Now he was about to send them not out in the world, but out into the far reaches of space. The probability was almost certain, he would never see them again. It was a bitter-sweet moment.

Kronkite was checking the chronometer when the two couples, Atom and Evelyn, Orwell and Darla, entered the sterile glass enclosure which protected them from microbial contamination. Everything was on schedule. Dressed in their bulky space gear, the four astronauts greeted Kronkite with a smile and a wave.

"Good morning," said Kronkite, returning their smiles and talking through the intercom. "Did you sleep well last night?"

"Yes, we finally slept. Although, mentally, we were very excited," replied Atom. "How are conditions for the liftoff?"

"So far, everything is favorable." Then Kronkite paused significantly. "Have any of you... misgivings? Any second thoughts about participating in this project?"

Atom turned to look in Evelyn's eyes. Each of the four exchanged inquiring glances.

"Well, sir," said Atom, after several seemingly long seconds, "I guess the silence says it all." As leader of the group, Atom normally spoke for the four of them. "So, if all systems are GO, sir, we're ready."

At that instant, Ames, the launch director, stepped forward. "Time for them to board, sir," he said quietly.

"Thank you, Ames," replied Kronkite as he looked into the face of each astronaut in turn.

"Atom, Evelyn, Orwell, Darla, it's a noble, brave, and magnanimous task you are assuming in setting out on this journey. All humanity is wishing you well. I wish I could shake hands with each of you."

The glass prevented any contact.

"Thank you, sir," said Atom, a dryness in his throat and his voice almost failing him.

"Evelyn, best wishes for a happy marriage from Sara and myself," offered Kronkite. "We want you to know that we're counting on you to keep things smooth and resolve any conflicts that may arise."

"I'll do my best to keep the peace. You may depend on it," replied Evelyn, adding "Please give my regards to Sara."

"Thank you, I will," said Kronkite. "Orwell, keep on acquiring knowledge. Your insights and efforts will be a boon to us all."

"Thanks, sir," returned Orwell, "I'll do my best to deserve your trust. And thanks for giving Darla and me this opportunity."

"You're very welcome, and deserving, I may add," said Kronkite.

Next, Kronkite turned to Orwell's wife. "Darla, your care, warmth, and concern, is vital to this undertaking. All my fervent hopes go with you."

"Finally, Atom, as leader of this expedition, I'll expect you to treat each member with equality and justice," said Kronkite. "Give them the same affection and respect that I feel for you. Remember that imperfections are natural, and only through accepting responsibility, not blaming others, can we improve ourselves. If there are any disputes, refer them to the Verity Scanner. At times, you may encounter excessive stress. Be patient, be compassionate, be vigilant. You must all work together. It must be a total team effort. Always remember the love we feel for you."

"We will, sir," said Atom, his voice filled with emotion. "I'll do my best. And I'm sure the others will do likewise."

With forced smiles and moist eyes, the four astronauts stepped into the gantry elevator. As Kronkite watched the elevator door close, a tear trickled down his cheek.

The elevator carried the silent and deeply-moved astronauts up to the top of the gantry. When the elevator door once again opened, they looked down the passageway that led to the open port of their spaceship, Starfarer. Darla and Evelyn were the first to enter, followed by Orwell and Atom.

"Shall we secure the port, Atom?" asked Director Ames.

"Yes" was the confident reply.

Gripping the solid entry door, the men pushed it shut and secured its fastenings. They were now doing routines they had many times rehearsed. In training, they had lightheartedly gone through the motions like play practice. Now they performed the same actions with serious intent and concentration.

Evelyn and Darla, who had preceded them, were already sitting in their launch seats, making the necessary attachments and securing their seat restraints. In front of them was the countdown clock which blinked rhythmically, moving time forward.

Atom made a visual check of their progress and then asked, "Any problems, anyone? Tell me if you have any." No problems were reported. Again, rehearsal smoothed the way.

Orwell and Atom settled into their launch seats and similarly attached themselves with connections and restraints. Each checked each other making certain all was completed.

"Time for the air check. Helmets, everyone," commanded Atom.

With the precision gained from repetition, the helmets were donned and made fast and all essential tests completed.

The launch headquarters checked their progress and confirmed every detail. The final countdown began.

Every nerve in Atom's body was alert, sensing, inquisitive. He listened to the control room checks as they were called off on the intercom. He monitored the instruments before him. "So, this is it," he thought. "One must be a complete fatalist to submit to such an undertaking as this— a complete fatalist... or... an idiot. Here I am sitting in a projectile fully tanked with explosive fuel. No time now to reconsider. No turning back now, unless the mission is aborted in the final countdown. I wonder what the others are thinking."

Atom looked back at his new bride. Evelyn gave him a shaky, but reassuring smile. He assumed all her senses were tense, too. For what? For malfunctions for which they had no control, no defense. He had to get a grip on himself. The stress and suspense was terrible.

He glanced over at Orwell. There was a gleam on his face. He appeared to be enjoying everything. He was drinking it all in. He had the expectant look of a child on a carnival ride. Did two years' difference in their age amount to that much? Certainly, Orwell was more the doer, more the risk-taker. He was probably imagining each relentless surge from fuel injection to ignition as it happened.

Atom wondered how Darla was doing. He looked back at her over his shoulder. She smiled back trustingly. She was the youngest of them all, and seemed to be holding up well. Still, who knows what someone else is thinking?

"Oh well," thought Atom, "if the Starfarer explodes, we'll never know the difference."

"Be patient," Kronkite had counseled. Easy to say, but the waiting seemed interminable and that's what Atom hated about it. He hated being out of control. He liked to be in command at all times and now several tons of rocketry and the tight grip of fate were boss.

Kronkite's thorough pre-liftoff checks were finally at an end.

"Ignition!" A thunderous roar from the huge launch rockets. A wave of vibration oscillated through the spaceship. Starfarer strained at its moorings as it developed thrust. The final countdown began: "10... 9... 8...."

Orwell turned to Atom. "The gantry is falling away." he said, as he mentally anticipated each step of the launch.

19

"7... 6... 5... 4..." The rumbling grew.
"Well, at last. This is really it," cheered Orwell.
"3... 2...."

CHAPTER III

"3...2...1... LIFTOFF!" The entire cycle was completed. The spaceship, Starfarer, straining against gravity, rose from the launch pad. With a rumbling roar and a burgeoning cloud of smoke it rose. A tremendous rush of adrenalin surged through the ground crew watching, tense and breathless, as the rocket arced into space.

Besides the crowd who ringed the launch site, the event was witnessed everywhere on TV. It was astonishing. It happened fast, and was quickly over. The spaceship shot into orbit and out-of-sight. Soaring from its planet of origin, it zoomed into space into an uncanny new form of reality. Freedom from gravity.

Atom and Evelyn, Orwell and Darla were heralded as envoys to space, cosmic colonists, couples of the future, pioneers whose quest was for a new galactic home for humanity. Kronkite's celebrity as the project leader paled in comparison. Of course, he was still revered as the inventor of the Verity Scanner. That would never change. But the Starfarer project was something else. It was natural that the couples had the spotlight. They had youth and vibrancy, and good looks in their favor. Also, it was their lives at risk. But what was the project all about? No one could quite say, not even Kronkite.

Vaguely, it became a river to ford, an ocean to cross, a continent to discover. You go there because it's there. Exploration for exploration's sake. But what if there was no hospitable other planet to find? What then? Was the project worth all the expenditure? If a habitable planet *was* found, could it save humanity in case of a world catastrophe? A climatic disaster? A rogue comet collision? A viral pandemic?

There were good people on both sides of the argument. While radio contact could be maintained, the benefits were clear-cut— a live presence light years away in the cosmos. The value to science was incalculable. The ability to perceive close at hand that which previously had only been a twinkle in a telescopic lens.

The Starfarer astronauts could perform some minimal analysis of stellar phenomenon and send back eyewitness reports. Close-up, they could observe planetary bodies which refractory distance obscured. Perhaps at last they could pierce the veil that concealed our place in the universe, grasp the nature, magnitude, and extent of the cosmos. It was heady stuff.

Others, with equal logic, argued that it was a shame to fund space exploration, even though it produced some employment, some technological development, some new knowledge. Hadn't there been sufficient progress already? Shouldn't the priority go to improving this planet, to increasing prosperity, to raising the education level of the poor? Why seek another planet when on this one so much was needed?

The arguments were valid on both sides and were very seldom joined. Each group of proponents had its area of expertise and influence, and its own coterie of followers. They did not socialize. And their advocates merely competed for funding. They both left the government budget hearings feeling somehow impoverished and not fully appreciated.

There was one vague, dreadful, almost incomprehensible, prospect which could unite the antagonists. That frightful prospect could be an impending destruction of the planet through some cataclysmic event— fire, flood, collision with a giant asteroid. Then the very survival of life might depend on migration to some other habitat, some other planet in the cosmos. In that event, Kronkite's space project would be unanimously applauded. There would be a clamor for more spaceships like Starfarer. It would become a universal obsession. A ticket on it would be worth millions. Minutes after Starfarer was safely airborne, Sara joined her husband and they embraced.

"You did it, dear! It was wonderful."

Kronkite expelled a sigh of relief. "Yes, they're safely on their way. Let's go to the communication room and see how our astronauts are doing."

As Sara and Kronkite walked through the jubilant control center, they were greeted with handshakes and pats on the back. The launch crew were all smiles. Kronkite praised his staff for their efforts. Then he and Sara went up to the communication room, a glassed-in booth within the immense crowded control center. An array of monitors covered a slightly curved wall. A larger screen displayed the progress of Starfarer. Kronkite greeted Ames, the launch director, at the console.

"How's reception?" asked Kronkite.

"Good. They're about to complete the post liftoff checklist," said Ames. "You'll be able to talk with them." A camera in Starfarer's pilot room gave Kronkite a view of the four astronauts strapped in their launch seats. They could have been four travelers in a car— the men in the front, the ladies in back— on an outing perhaps headed for the seashore or the mountains. Just like ordinary vacationers, except their self-contained vehicle weighed several thousands of tons.

"Darla, can you hear me?" asked Kronkite. The four astronauts all looked up toward the camera.

Orwell glanced back at Darla, and then waved at the camera.

"Yes, we can hear you loud and clear, sir," said Darla. Each of the astronauts was responsible for one major specialization for which he or she had received extensive training. Darla's specialty was communication.

"How do you feel?" Sara asked.

"Like I'm flying. And I mean that literally and figuratively," said Darla. "To think I used to get sick to my stomach on amusement park rides."

"How do you feel now?" said Kronkite, beginning to feel the irony of carrying on such a commonplace conversation as if they were in the same room, when actually they were separated by thousands of miles

"I have to admit," said Darla, smiling wryly, "I held my breath at the end of the countdown, but now feel great."

"How about the rest of you?" Kronkite asked.

"I feel the same way," said Evelyn. "Words are inadequate to describe it."

"The Mach Force was really something, sir. Now I really know what it means to be glued to one's seat," chuckled Orwell. "Booster rocket separation was much smoother than I expected."

"Well, now that Starfarer has stabilized, it's time for your new condition – weightlessness."

"Atom perhaps you should go first. It takes time getting used to," said Kronkite. "Release your strap restraints carefully so they don't fly... or you yourself, for that matter."

"Okay, here goes, sir." Atom gingerly pushed the releases. He immediately sensed how each exertion could be exaggerated. Suddenly, he was aloft, floating like a gas balloon. It was like being a bird without wings to maneuver with.

"It'll take some getting used to," said Kronkite. "A little practice and you'll master it."

"Wow, this is wild," said Atom, free-floating over the heads of the others who, giggling, watched him bob overhead like a birthday balloon. He felt elated but awkward, like a child taking its first baby steps. There was a gangling feeling to it that for Atom, who always liked to be in control, was uncomfortable. He adapted, but not without suppressing some embarrassment. Atom managed to press the ceiling and right himself.

"You'll catch on," encouraged Kronkite who could only see Atom's feet floating at the top of his monitor. "That's why I suggest that you only unbuckle one at a time," he added. "That way you'll avoid colliding."

Atom gently propelled himself from the ceiling down the wall of the small pilot room. Finally, at last he was able to position himself by the side of Evelyn.

"May I have this dance," he asked, "with my new bride?"

Evelyn laughed and blushed like a freshman at a prom.

"Push your releases carefully and I'll help you." Atom was never more attentive than when he was being cavalier.

Soon, all the astronauts were swimming in the air of the pilot room while Kronkite, Sara, and the communication room personnel watched their antics on the monitor like viewers of a comedy show. Orwell amused everyone walking on his head. His act added a tinge of surrealism to the scene.

"Now that you're somewhat adjusted to your new air-borne freedom," said Kronkite, smiling at Orwell's antics, "I must be serious for a moment. You understand we will continue controlling your flight for the time being, and the early part of your journey. Starfarer will be on autopilot. Atom, of course, you will always be in charge. You may take control over autopilot at any time. We will go through some tests in future days. So, you may experience the actual control over the autopilot."

"Other than emergencies, there will be times when, at your discretion, you will also take over control from autopilot to reset Starfarer's course. Orwell, Evelyn, Darla, you'll be informed of any flight pattern or course changes. I think this was all thoroughly covered in your preliminary instruction," said Kronkite with his usual efficiency. "I think it should be repeated for the sake of clarity."

"Now it's time to go through your further post-launch checklist."

Atom, who was nearest to the instruction file, reached for the checkers and floated the devices to each of the astronauts. It was comical to see them dealt out with more ease than a casino card dealer. The four of them were still attired in their suits and helmets each of which contained an air supply. It was necessary to pressure check the spaceship against acceleration stress or vibration damage. This was essential to establish the integrity of the hull and their self-contained atmosphere. One by one, they rode the elevator tube from the pilot house into the main gallery and gym.

In the gallery, the astronauts looked like divers swimming in the hull of a ship. Orwell and Darla took the port hallway to examine the living and recreation room. Atom and Evelyn turned right into the starboard hallway to examine the auxiliary control room and the data library computer room. Next, the couples examined their own staterooms and privies. On the next level down, Atom and Sara checked the lab and sick bay while Orwell and Darla checked the dining room next to the gallery.

Kronkite and the ground crew watched the monitor as the astronauts traversed the spaceship and came into view at various fixed camera locations. When everything checked out, the astronauts would look into the camera lens and give a thumbs-up. Finally, the couples met in the greenhouse.

"Everything check out on the port side?" asked Atom.

"Port's okay. This is like floating in a fishbowl, isn't it?" chuckled Orwell, mimicking a fish.

"Yeah," agreed Atom, propelling himself topsy-turvy along, "except I'm not as graceful as a fish. This goes against anything I was ever taught. I was always told in order to get ahead, to keep both feet on the ground."

Joined by Darla, Evelyn scrutinized the greenhouse. As the plant physiologist on the team, Evelyn was particularly interested in how the containerized plants had weathered takeoff into space. Some leaves and debris were floating like autumn leaves, but much more languidly. It would all settle once the gravity kicked in. She was well aware of the task awaiting her and assumed the responsibility with excitement and enthusiasm.

Besides her duties, Evelyn planned an experiment to grow plants in weightless space in a little section of the pilot house. She would pioneer in space agriculture. This opportunity would make her the first space horticulturist. She'd have assistance, but it would be her bailiwick. Her field of expertise was especially significant since the greenhouse provided the food and oxygen for the spaceship. As Evelyn and Darla floated from plant to plant, it was almost as if they were hummingbirds darting from blossom to blossom. Indeed, if the bees, now shut up in their hives, didn't work out in space. Then it would be necessary in the future for all the plants to be cross-pollinated by hand.

Meanwhile, Atom and Orwell went below to examine the oxy-carbo-dioxide exchanger. They took readings and checked them against specs. Orwell watched after air mixtures. His special study was devoted to internal systems and electronic circuitry and, most important, Starfarer's atmosphere.

Atom's specialization was navigation, rocketry, and ionic propulsion. Plus, the Quantum Time Compressor. During the journey, each astronaut was to instruct the others about his or her area of expertise. There was much to learn. This would be their only backup. Otherwise, they would have to rely on the ground crew's advice or computerized service manuals.

"Tolerances must remain in these calibrations," said Orwell as he showed the system to Atom.

"You modify the pressures by the corresponding valves." Orwell pointed to the proper air controls.

Atom listened to Orwell's explanation and studied the air exchange intently. "What if there was a great deviation in those readings?" asked Atom.

"We'd be in deep trouble, that's what. Quickly, we'd have to put on our auxiliary air masks. Except for air failure, explosion, or massive puncture of the ships exterior, that's not likely to happen. Most of these are internally controlled by computer. Besides, if any of these gauges deviate beyond the acceptable tolerance, an alarm will sound. It should give us ample warning to correct the problem."

"Fine," said Atom. "That's good to know."

"Yes, it all checks out," said Orwell, adding, "We'll be able to doff our space togs now."

Atom and Orwell propelled their way through the starboard passageway. They met Evelyn and Darla floating, still weightless, waiting for them in the main gallery. They felt somewhat giddy from their flying inspection. The weightless experience had proved to be quite amusing.

"Everything stern checked out," said Atom. "How's things forward?"

"All's copacetic," said Darla.

They re-entered the pilot room by way of the elevator tube and removed their helmets. For the first time in space they breathed their new atmosphere and it was good. Then they assisted each other with the clumsy task of removing their bulky space suits in their weightless environment. Atom hung up each suit and helmet in the closet adjacent to the sealed chamber door through which they had entered Starfarer from the gantry.

Back on home base, Kronkite's brow un-furrowed as he sensed a good report coming. A serious malfunction could have aborted the project. The launch crew and people all over the globe were glued to their television sets with expectancy and fascination. There was universal interest in the project.

Atom hung up the last helmet. Concealed in the closet were four special plastic drinking vessels which he had hidden prior to the launch. He handed a glass to each of his fellow astronauts and they turned to face the camera which was transmitting their images to ground control.

"Can you hear us, Kronkite?" asked Atom facing the camera directly.

"Loud and clear," Kronkite replied.

"Dedicated project crew, friends, and citizens everywhere, please accept this our toast to you," said Atom as they raised their cups. "We are all made of star-stuff, and so it is most fitting that we set out on this journey— the first space colonists from our planet. Your efforts have opened the door to the cosmos. We enter it gladly with hope and aspiration soaring. Our love and gratitude to you all for making it possible. And to you, Kronkite, Sara, and citizens everywhere, we especially promise never ever to be *myth-informed*. And we're not lisping when we say that."

The toast made, the astronauts raised their cups. Hearing Kronkite's old joke repeated, there followed rollicking laughter all around.

"Thank you, Atom and astronauts," said Kronkite laughing most heartily of all.

On this momentous occasion, there was a great deal of satisfaction with the project for both those in space and on the ground. The launch had succeeded admirably.

*   *   *

Thus, the Starfarer voyage began. It was the culmination of the new Verity Scanner culture. It was a new era of manufacturing. The Scanner had produced a new work ethic. Quality was no longer a matter of cost. It was a matter of care. Craftsmanship became the watchword. Designers, builders, and workers were measured by truthfulness. Nothing was to be gained by fakery. Pride, thus self-esteem, could be gained only by being scrupulously honest with oneself and with others.

In the past, self-delusion had been very prevalent. That had to be overcome. Now questions were valued above all, and all things were subject to question. Crooked profiteers and labor racketeers could no longer worm their way into industry. The Verity Scanner ruthlessly rooted them out. Eliminating workplace rip-offs, quality increased, followed by increased prosperity for the whole population. New standards arose for durability, efficiency, and efficacy. Waste in the society was decreased by making better products, less energy-wasting products.

Competition still existed, but competitors were judged on merit. Teamwork improved with honesty. An essential element for the Starfarer project to succeed would be cooperation.

Days passed as Atom and Evelyn, Orwell and Darla, adapted to their new lives. The ground crew continued monitoring Starfarer's progress. Kronkite and Sara followed the spaceship daily, often bringing in packed lunches so they could remain at the console in the communications room.

At six, Sara reflected back on Atom's speech. "That was a wonderful toast he made, wasn't it?"

"Yes, it was. Quite poetic for someone as reserved as Atom."

"While he was giving it, I snuck a peek at what commentators were saying on television. It caused quite a stir. People were dancing in the streets."

"Is that right?" Kronkite grinned. "That's wonderful. Think of that. Everyone everywhere sharing the joy of progress. Marvelous."

"Now that it's over do you feel a bit letdown?"

"No, only relief," he said, enjoying a tasty bite.

"I'm glad. You haven't forgotten your promise?"

At this, a flush came over Kronkite's face. A look of puzzlement at Sara's question.

27

"Remember? You promised to treat us to a much-deserved *unbridled* vacation."

"You're right," conceded Kronkite. I did."

"Well...?"

A tortured helpless look spread over Kronkite's face. "That's still one of the world's ills. Good intentions make the damnedest liars. I had fully intended it at the time. But... while we're in contact with Starfarer.... Oh, darling, will you forgive me if we postpone our vacation till Starfarer is out of reach of our radio range?"

Sara looked at her husband with mocked annoyance, then sighed. "Of course. It's no different than what I expected. I didn't think you'd be able to leave the project yet, even after all this time."

Kronkite reached across the table and held her hand. "We'll have that vacation. And that's a Verity Scanner promise. Now we'd better get some sleep. Tomorrow is *gravity* day."

CHAPTER IV

That night, while Sara and Kronkite slept, the Starfarer explorers gazed out from the lofty vantage point of their spaceship at their former rotating birthplace. It was a glorious sight. It was a fascinating sight. It filled them with nostalgia. Their eyes took in the globe's seas, its continents, its swirling atmosphere of clouds. Like children in a toy store, they looked and pointed and chattered with delight as they recognized familiar geographic features. The blue-green sphere was like an exotic emerald spinning in coal-black space. It was a sight they wanted to imprint into memory forever. It was a sight they would soon leave behind.

They had eaten their prepackaged meal in the pilot room. After all the excitement of the launch, the astronauts were exhausted. They fell asleep.

The ground crew on night shift monitored their orbit. Soon, the astronauts would be settling into their alternating duty shifts, but for now, they slept together. It would be the last time of the journey that they did so.

As dawn came up, Kronkite was back at the control headquarters to oversee the final step before Starfarer's free flight into the void. The final step was to engage the centrifugal gravity.

"Good morning…Did you sleep well?" asked Kronkite over the intercom.

The astronauts were waking and stretching.

"I slept as sound as a cat," said Atom.

"Yeah," said Orwell. "I call this really light sleeping. Unless tied down, you float away."

"Then you must be ready for gravity," said Kronkite.

"You mean you want us to give up our wings already?" quipped Orwell.

They all smiled and chatted amiably as the ground crew prepared for the next procedure.

The conical pilot house in which the astronauts sat was in the bow. It was attached to a long center shaft which extended to the stern and the propelling rockets. Enclosed in this shaft midway down was a gyroscopic stabilizer. Surrounding the shaft was an immense cylinder which contained the living quarters for the astronauts. These compartments from bow to stern were divided into rooms. In shape, the cylinder resembled a roll from a paper towel dispenser. The pilot room was the only room not in the cylinder.

Between the pilothouse and gallery was a tubular elevator shaft. The astronauts had jokingly dubbed this elevator "the can" because it was shaped like a large tin-can. Inside it, were straps and grips with which to secure oneself. When it descended, a clutch engaged so that it gradually took on the rotation of the main gallery room into which it entered.

Each section of the cylinder was designated a zone and was given a number. Zone one was the main gallery and gym. Except for the greenhouse, this was Starfarer's most spacious room. The purpose of the main gallery and gym was to provide an area for movement and physical exercise. It also served as a contrast and relief to the more cramped and confining compartments. On the room wall were exercisers to keep the astronauts physically fit.

Next to the gallery was Zone two. In this zone was the auxiliary control room with its numerous monitors, intercoms, and navigational controls. It also served as the radio shack. Two Verity Scanners were stored inside a cabinet. The flight controls were duplicates of those found in Starfarer's conical bow pilot cabin. Next to the control room also in the Zone two, was the living and recreation room. The hallways were two passageways connecting the gallery to the greenhouse. Thus, Zone five could be reached without passing through the middle zones and without entering any of the command rooms.

Each zone compartment could be sealed and isolated by doors to protect the interior atmosphere, if necessary. This was a precaution against asteroid damage. Zone three contained the astronaut's staterooms. And Zone four consisted of the dining room, galley, and the lab and sickbay. Although structure and function mandated the room shapes, there was an attempt on the part of the designers to incorporate some color aesthetics on interior walls. Very much like a cruise ship.

Finally, in Zone five was the all-important spacious greenhouse. The entire spaceship was dependent upon this large area, since it provided the oxygen and food to sustain life. In essence, Starfarer was a giant flying greenhouse.

In order to create an artificial gravity, the large cylinder containing all the living quarters had to rotate on the central rocket axis. The four astronauts sat in their launch seats waiting for the rotation to begin. The spinning had to gain speed gradually in order not to destabilize the rocket.

"All seat restraints secured?" inquired Ames from ground control.

"All secured," confirmed Atom.

"Very well. On the count of three, release the spin brakes."

"3... 2... 1... rotation commenced."

At the end of the count, Atom released the brakes which permitted the cylinder to start rotation. The astronauts felt a slight wobble as the procedure began. All were tense. This was the test flight. They would soon know if the design would function properly. Atom held his breath. He was concerned whether he could keep the rocket stable with a minimum of adjustment.

"Let 'er rip," said Orwell, who was thrilled with the whole process.

"That's just like you," said Darla, who was reminded of their teen-age dates at carnivals, when Orwell would rock the seats on the rides and make her shriek.

"Don't worry, honey," Orwell would chide, "we're perfectly safe."

Out the side ports, they could see their cylindrical home picking up speed while the pilot room remained constant.

"Gravity established," announced Ames over the radio from land base.

Kronkite stood silently in the ground control room observing. He rubbed his hands with satisfaction to see the cylinder rotate as planned. He could hardly wait to see the astronauts try it out.

"Are you ready to test your new gravity?" radioed Kronkite.

"You bet, sir" replied Atom unbuckling his seat restraints. Take over the controls, Orwell, and no loop-de-loops," Atom kidded.

Orwell looked at Atom and smiled. "Don't worry, I can fly straight when I want to."

Atom floated weightless through the air of the pilot room back to "the can", their tube elevator. He entered it, strapped himself in, and held on to the grips. When it descended, a clutch engaged so that it gradually took on the motion of the main gallery into which it entered. Atom unbuckled and wiggled out of "the can" into the platform and climbed down the ladder to experience his first gravity since launch day.

From the camera in the gallery, Kronkite watched Atom take his first steps on artificial gravity.

"How is it?" asked Kronkite over the gallery speaker, watching Atom from the area's monitor.

"Strange sensation, but it works?" said Atom. "It'll be fine, once I get my sea legs."

Next to join Atom using the tube elevator was Evelyn, followed by Darla and finally, Orwell. Starfarer was now on auto-pilot. They hugged and congratulated each other as they experienced their new gravity for the first time. The four walked around the gallery/gym adjusting to their new walking condition and occasionally trying out some of the exercise equipment.

"These weights are great," said Orwell. "I'll be able to keep in shape."

The ground crew watched them get accustomed to the new gravity over the monitors.

"How do you like it, Evelyn?" asked Kronkite.

"It takes a little getting used to," she answered.

"Yeah," said Darla. "My eyes tell me I'm walking uphill, but my legs don't feel it."

"Just imagine," chuckled Orwell, "we're climbing up the ceiling like a fly, but it must look like we're only moving on a treadmill like a hamster."

"I wish I was there to experience it with you," said Kronkite.

"We wish you were, too," Atom replied.

"That's the trouble with being an old dog like me," Kronkite said. "You miss out on all the newest stuff."

The astronauts had, of course, seen all Starfarer's interiors on the ground, though not in a weightless state. Now they were walking in the spaceship with artificial gravity. What had been walls and ceiling was now floor. It was so different in aspect that they explored the rooms and facilities hand-in-hand like new home owners. Conversion to centrifugal gravity was a success. Another feather in Kronkite's cap.

Later at home-base noon, the couples met in their dining room for their first meal with their new artificial gravity. As they were sitting at the table eating, Atom said "Here's the schedule that Kronkite made out for us. It's a twelve-hour swing shift. Which shift do you and Darla want?"

"Why don't we take the first work-shift," said Darla to Orwell smiling and slyly winking, "and let the newlyweds have the first rest period." "Does that suit you two?" asked Orwell.

"Evelyn?"

"Fine with me, Atom," said Evelyn.

"Okay, then that's settled. We'll join you at six which will be our breakfast and your dinner. So, till then...." Atom took Evelyn by the hand. They walked out through the galley into the hall walking from Zone four to Zone three. When they arrived at their stateroom door, Atom swept Evelyn up into his arms. "Welcome to your new home, sweetheart." Evelyn murmured and smiled and kissed him as he carried her into their room and closed the door.

There were no cameras in the staterooms or privies so the couple's activities were not monitored on the ground control screens.

*   *   *

Five hours later, the couples met back at the galley dining room.

"You look refreshed," said Orwell to Atom and Evelyn. "Don't you think they look refreshed, Darla?"

The four of them sat down and ate. Atom and Evelyn had breakfast, and Orwell and Darla ate dinner. From this time on, they would alternate these two meals at twelve hour intervals.

Later at nine while Atom was examining his navigation charts in Zone two control room, Orwell walked up to him. "Atom, would you have any objection to Darla and I sleeping in the pilot room tonight?"

"The pilot room?" said Atom surprised. "Want to watch the stars, do you?"

"Something like that. But don't view me through the Verity Scanner, all right?"

That night, the ground crew's pilot room monitor went blank. First, they suspected an electrical malfunction. Actually, what they didn't know was, Orwell had covered the lens so he and Darla could try a little weightless romantic flying. It was the first time anyone could genuinely say 'Love was in the air.'

CHAPTER V

The Starfarer project was both natural and unnatural. It was natural in that most creatures have members who migrate to other groups or areas. It was unnatural in that the ordinary tendency for groups or individuals is to cling to the safety of the known and familiar.

Is there a biological component to such behavior? If so, what explains it?

The cat family is territorial, as are many bird species. Deer herd together with bucks contesting for dominance. Bears live individual lives after weaning and separation. Bees colonize by swarming.

Among the public, the space project generated a good deal of shared excitement. Yet the phenomenon of migration and colonization remained little understood. Some migrate for change of climate. Other migrations result from population pressure, or a need for food, or the desire for personal betterment, or even perhaps, fame, curiosity, maybe even to seek treasure. The reason for Starfarer was difficult to pin down.

Perhaps its impetus was Kronkite, his vision, his curiosity, his ambition that made him the charismatic leader that he was.

The technical element was definitely Kronkite. The inventor of the Verity Scanner was a genius of the possible. He knew how to get results from physical reality and phenomenon. He knew how to gather and appraise knowledge and make it do his bidding. He was a stickler for facts. He had no use for ancient hand-me-down thinking. Not that he didn't revere enlightened ancestors who had brought progress and advanced civilization. It was those who wallowed in mythical darkness that he abhorred.

Unless Kronkite had incontrovertible evidence, he suspended belief. Nothing less would do.

On the other hand, as a psychologist, Sara dealt with the less tangible, more variable attributes of personality. Heredity, environment, conditioning, motivation, relationships, health, stress, circumstances, all were factors affecting her study of the always fluid and unpredictable human character.

In the laboratory, Kronkite could test the temper of metals. He could check their molecular structure for durability, flexibility, and tensile strength. Experimentally, it was not as easy for Sara to check the human

34

mind. Nonetheless, she had made a lot of progress in identifying character traits by using the Verity Scanner and her own specially developed CHARM QUOTA Personality Test.

Kronkite and Sara cooperated as husband and wife. As a research team, they were both optimistic and believed in progress and improvement. Kronkite strove to eliminate flaws in materials, electronics, and mechanical apparatus which could result from inept design or faulty human decisions. He did not believe men and women should be robotized, and neither did Sara. In their opinion, attempts to take away human freedom always resulted in tyranny and disaster. Always, the greedy and narcissistic seek to destroy freedom and subjugate others in order only to glorify themselves.

So, for Kronkite and Sara, it was a kind of race— technical perfectibility versus human perfectibility. Kronkite was working on one side of the equation, and Sara, the other. It was not an easy task— a one truth— as advocated by simple-minded dogmatists. One truth without diversity was not diversity at all. Without diversity, freedom could not exist. Freedom and diversity means that humans would always have to think, and examine, and question, and make studied logical decisions. Sloth in reasoning automatically meant forfeiture of freedom.

With navigation equipment, perfection means steering a safe course and arriving at a desired destination. Human perfection was not so different from this except humans needed satisfaction with the journey. That is where Sara came into the Starfarer program.

She created the CHARM QUOTA Personality Test that was used in the selection of the astronauts for the Starfarer project. The test was divided into two parts: past performance and personality traits. The first part, past performance, was designated by the acronym CHARM, which stood for *Character, Honesty, Achievement, Reasoning ability, and Manners.* These characteristics could be confirmed by checking the Verity Scanner Reputation File.

The second part, which Sara's test examined, was personality traits. These traits were designated by the acronym QUOTA: *Quick, Unselfish, Optimistic, Tenacious, and Accommodating.* From all who took these tests, Sara and Kronkite had selected Atom, Evelyn, Orwell and Darla.

Atom's character suggested he strove to please and wanted to succeed. Perhaps because his parents were killed in an auto accident when he was four and a half, he was attracted to the Starfarer project unconsciously seeking a parent. Kronkite became his father figure. Eagerly, Atom sought to serve him, to please him, to win his praise. The dispassionate, childless Kronkite filled this role, but only partly. Which was most important to Kronkite, the relationship or the project? One wondered.

Nonetheless, of the thirty-eight candidates, Kronkite chose Atom. The young man's engagement to Evelyn hadn't hurt his being chosen either. She was one of the stars of the training program— bright and eminently qualified with her degree in plant physiology. Their marriage on the eve of the launch was an angle news reporters jumped at. Headlines read: ASTRONAUT COUPLE TO TAKE HONEYMOON TRIP IN SPACE!

Curiously, the younger couple chosen, Orwell and Darla, were nearing their second anniversary. They were childhood sweethearts and had entered the Starfarer training program together. An important fact of their selection was that their skills complimented Atom's and Evelyn's.

Seven the next morning, the astronauts, after eating their respective breakfasts and dinners, were sitting in the pilothouse. They had been orbiting their former world barely restrained by the invisible umbilical cord— gravity. Now they were about to cut this tether and fly off into space.

"Good morning or good evening, whichever fits," said Kronkite at the ground console. "How is everything?"

"Just fine," answered Atom to Kronkite's transmitted voice.

"How are the plants, Evelyn? Much launch damage?"

"Relatively little. They are quite tenacious. As a matter of fact, they are adapting very well. I've already begun some new plantings earlier today."

"That's good. Ames reports that all readings are within proper parameters. Orwell, are you ready to leave orbit?"

"Can't wait, sir. I'm looking forward to our first close-up of our planetary system. By the way, did you see the game last night? You might say I had a bird's eye view of it," chuckled Orwell.

"No. I didn't see it."

"Oh well, I watched it all in the recreation room. Looks like Mayberry will be picked for the most valuable player award."

"Yeah, I watched it, too," piped in Ames at the console. "I think Fernwood still has a chance in the playoffs."

"Sorry to say, I don't follow sports much," said Kronkite. "Sara always complains that I don't have enough interests outside of my work, don't you, darling?"

Sara smiled and gave Kronkite a mock look of disgust. "Is that my only choice? Playing second fiddle to your work or being a sport's widow?"

"I hope not," laughed Kronkite. "A word of advice to both of you guys — never promise your wife anything until you're ready to deliver. She won't let you forget, believe me. Isn't that so?"

"That's right, dear. You know by now that a wife has a longer memory than a computer."

"Sara," asked Evelyn, "since I'm new at this, do they always deliver?"

"They'd better," answered Sara, "or peace goes out the window."

"In that case, I better collect a few promises," smiled Evelyn with a raised eyebrow at Atom.

They all chuckled at the banter.

Atom smiling, changed the subject. "Is it set? Is outer space still clocked for 08:00?" he asked.

"08:06, to be precise," said Ames, "within a range of plus or minus 0:02. Accuracy will maximize the targeted trajectory and minimize fuel consumption, of course."

For the remainder of the orbit, the astronauts and ground crew chatted amiably while attending to their instruments. Sometimes the astronauts drifted into silent reverie as they watched the birth home they were leaving— the home that slowly spun beneath them all colorfully dressed: land, oceans and clouds.

Atom reached back and gave Evelyn's hand a squeeze. Orwell looked back at Darla with a great big grin. "Boy, this is going to make astronomy real," he said.

At exactly 08:06, the spaceship's rockets fired, and Starfarer, with its four passengers aboard, shot out of orbit into the measureless immensity of space!

CHAPTER VI

The astronauts severed bonds with their world. They were shooting through space, a mere speck in the cosmos. They were leaving behind all that was familiar, all that was known, all that was certain. They were leaving home. Their spaceship, Starfarer, was speeding away from their birthplace toward the vastness of space. More than a comet, they were free to roam. They were flying into aerie infinity. Their destination: a different planet, a new home somewhere out among thousands of points of light. Perhaps to a new star system, a different galaxy.

Each working shift, the couples busied themselves with routine living, maintenance and chores: food preparation, farming in the greenhouse, observations, navigation, daily communication with Kronkite. Little time was devoted to recreation of any kind. Only Orwell spent some of his time watching television. He liked sports. And TV was still accessible. For the most part, the astronauts were endlessly busy, working, and rest was always needed and welcome.

When she wasn't busy in communication with ground control, Darla had been checking various frequencies for signals emanating from far out in space. For several years, she had been associated with a project the members called ROSS. The name of the group was *Radio Outer Space Scanners*. It was their hope and purpose to establish radio contact with life in outer space. Each day she sent out messages and checked for responses. So far, she had nothing to report. The fact that she was involved in ROSS was a distinct plus for Darla and Orwell when the selection for the Starfarer crew was made.

One morning, Darla suffered from some queasiness which she interpreted as motion sickness. She was inclined to have it, so it didn't surprise her. It was the first she had experienced since embarkation. She took some tablets which Kronkite had provided and stayed in bed.

That morning, Darla didn't feel like eating. She didn't even want to be near food. Orwell, Evelyn, and Atom met in the dining room and sat down at the table to eat together.

"Sorry Darla doesn't feel better," said Evelyn. "It could be stress from after the launch."

"That's all right. She'll get over it. She always does," said Orwell.

Changing the subject, Atom, in one of his reflective moods, asked, "What do you think contributes most to progress and advancement?" Atom liked table topics.

After some thought, Evelyn spoke. "I say books."

"No, it's got to be inventions," countered Orwell.

"Those are both good," thought Atom, "but what about exploration, or imagination, or experimentation, or...."

"Or leadership," interrupted Orwell.

"Exploration and experimentation are all recorded in books," said Evelyn.

"So are inventions," said Orwell, "but they're also manufactured and have an impact on civilization."

"Without imagination, exploration, or experimentation, there wouldn't be any books or even inventions," said Atom.

"True," agreed Evelyn, "but it's only when ideas are shared that they have any impact. Books disseminate ideas. Books take ideas across oceans."

"So does television," said Orwell. "Sure, it takes imagination to see the application of something new to something useful, but it's only when a new invention is developed that progress occurs," insisted Orwell.

"Still, most advancement comes first from ideas. So, ideas come first. Ideas recorded in books, for example."

"But Evelyn," objected Orwell, "ideas can lead people astray. Fanatics acting on imagined racial or religious superiority create hatred and cause conflict and war and...and other atrocities. That's why proper leadership is necessary for progress."

"But is it the imaginary ideas themselves, or the leaders who foment them that are most at fault?" asked Atom.

"I think it would have to be both equally," said Evelyn. "Ideas influence leaders and leaders push ideas."

Orwell leaned forward triumphantly. "That's why inventions contribute more to advancement than books or leaders. Inventions are not imaginary and they're neutral."

"However, are they totally neutral?" wondered Atom.

"What do you mean?"

"War weapons are inventions, but are they neutral? Do they contribute to progress? After all, guns used for hunting, end up being used to kill people."

Orwell leaned back and pursed his lips. "Well, new technology has also resulted from weapon research. And besides, the purpose of weapons is for defense."

"Not always. Leaders don't always use weapons for defense. Much of

39

the time, weapons are used for invasion or terrorism," said Atom. "And, I may add, often to suppress freedom."

"That was before Kronkite invented the Verity Scanner. Isn't that right?" pushed Orwell. "It took a superior invention to lead to that advancement. Can you argue against that?"

"Orwell's got a point there, sweetheart," said Evelyn.

"I have to admit, it's hard to argue against Kronkite's Verity Scanner," said Atom.

"And," continued Orwell, "books, which are largely the reflection of the past, could hardly affect civilization in the same way that the Verity Scanner has— an invention, mind you. Oh, and I know what you're going to say."

"What?" smiled Atom affably.

"Without Kronkite's leadership, the Verity Scanner would not exist. But I contend that it's not the inventor but the invention that has the major effect on society."

"Your point is well taken," said Atom. "So, here we are headed for a new planet, perhaps a new galaxy. What is the greatest gift we bring with us? Is it books, knowledge, exploration, the Verity Scanner or maybe ourselves? What do you think?"

"You're forgetting one thing... maybe more than one thing," said Evelyn.

"What's that?" asked Atom, trying to think what might have been missed.

"Plants!" she said emphatically. "You mustn't forget plants." Evelyn pronounced the words with an air of satisfaction.

Orwell giggled at her triumph.

Atom smiled. "Of course, you're absolutely right," he said. "In all of space, plants are extremely valuable and have added immensely to the richness of lives. As a matter of fact, life wouldn't be the same without them. That's for sure. Our lives are vastly improved by the addition of new food sources and products from plants. It makes me shudder to think how defoliation of large areas back home took place before preventive action was taken."

Evelyn picked up some dishes. "That reminds me. I think we'd better leave that topic for another mealtime. I've work to do in the greenhouse."

"Do you need any help, sweetheart? Can I give you a hand after I check on navigation?"

"Oh, you honeymooners," mused Orwell. "Well, I'm going to see how Darla's feeling. And then, since it's my recreation time, I'll go watch last night's game. See you later."

Evelyn went directly to tend the plants in the greenhouse, while Atom went to the auxiliary navigation room. From there he could view outside using video camera's which were strategically placed. He could pan, tilt, and zoom the cameras even to the exterior of Starfarer. He studied the screen. Ahead was the eternal night of space with its sprinkling of star lights. Behind, he could see their fleeing world. He was astonished to see how soon its size had diminished. He looked at it wistfully, like an old photograph in an album. Next, he checked his bearings. Starfarer was on course, on autopilot. He left closing the control room door.

Going down the passageway, he stopped at Orwell and Darla's bedroom. He paused, pondering whether or not to knock. Finally, he tapped lightly on the door. "If Darla was asleep, maybe he wouldn't wake her," Atom thought.

"Yes," came Darla's voice from within. "Who is it?"

"Atom," he said musing quietly to himself. The question struck him absurdly. On the Starfarer how many choices were there?

"Oh, Atom," she said. "Come in."

Atom opened the door and looked in. "I was wondering how you were feeling?"

Pillow propped behind her, Darla was sitting up in bed. Although she was wearing a nightie, she held the sheet shyly up over her breasts.

"Something I ate must not have agreed with me," she said.

"Sorry to hear that. If you like, I'll take over your ROSS radio stint later."

"Thanks, but that won't be necessary. I should be up and about by then. I'm feeling better already. My stomach only made me miss my recreation time."

Gazing at Darla snuggled in her bed, Atom was moved by her beauty and femininity. They had spent a good deal of time together, but were always dressed in their uniform space duds which tended to neuter a person.

"Well, if you need anything, just call. I'll be down in the greenhouse."

"Thanks, I will," said Darla.

Atom nodded and closed the door. He walked through the passageway and entered the greenhouse. The humid air had a freshness and a bite to it. It swelled his nostrils. The greenery flooded the mind with memories of going outdoors at home.

Atom walked along the greenhouse corridor surrounded by plants. He came up to Evelyn undetected. She was observing some yellow blossoms very closely. From behind, he put his arm around her and kissed her lovingly on the nape of her neck… She didn't jump, but she was pleasantly surprised.

"Mm-m," she sighed, "that sent a shiver up and down me."

They embraced tenderly. When Atom grew more amorous, Evelyn held him off. "Better not here, sweetie," she said.

"Why? Because your darling plants are watching?"

"No. Because Orwell might come in and... besides, don't forget the greenhouse cameras. Do you know where they're mounted? I keep forgetting where they are. I don't think we want to make the six o'clock news back home. Let's keep our private business, private. Hadn't we better?"

"Oh yes. I almost forgot. The ground crew." Atom laughed giving Evelyn a warm hug.

"Let me show you something," she said, disentangling herself from the warmth of his arms. "Look here." She pointed to the bell-shaped yellow blossoms. At first, Atom wondered what she meant, and then he saw. A bee was busily gathering pollen from the pistil and stamen of the flower.

"I released the bees this morning. They appear to be adapting nicely. It's a great worry off my mind. I was afraid I might have to do all the pollinating myself. Bees are such good workers. I'm so grateful to them."

"I can see why you're so happy, and I'm happy for you, believe me," said Atom. "Do you think that plants— flowers in particular— feel passion as much as we do, my dear plant doctor?"

"I don't know about that, but I think you can credit their flower power for creating a lot of passion," laughed Evelyn. "Isn't it time for a break?"

"Why, yes, it is," agreed Atom checking his watch. "Let's not keep the bees from their good work." They left the greenhouse. On their way, they met Orwell coming from the recreation room. There was a look of displeasure on his face.

"Ever notice how when you're congratulating yourself on everything going right— something goes wrong?"

"Why? What happened?" asked Atom.

"I thought Mayberry was a sure thing for best ball player. Then he goes and sprains an ankle, and it looks like Fernwood will get the MVP instead."

"That's the breaks, I guess," said Atom, relieved it wasn't a problem affecting Starfarer.

"There is some good news that may make you feel better," said Evelyn.

"Oh, what's that?" Orwell asked.

"The bees are working, so we should get some honey."

"That *is* good news. Well, I'm off to see how Darla is feeling. I'll tell her about the bees, although she's always been afraid of them."

"We're heading back to our room, too," said Atom, "to get refreshed. Tell Darla not to worry about the bees. See you later."

CHAPTER VII

It was amazing, but nonetheless, true. When the astronauts looked back at their home now, it was barely a speck of light. All that hustle and bustle, all that traveling back and forth, all that endless eating and chattering, all that laughing and crying, all that loving and hating, now nothing but a pinpoint of light.

After twelve days and millions of miles, they were rendezvousing with their nearest planet neighbor.

They had no great expectations for the first encounter. Astronomers concluded long ago that it was a desolate body incapable of supporting life. Therefore, it was not a candidate for colonization.

Some highly imaginative astronomer, in peering through his telescope, had thought he detected roads, buildings, and monuments. Like a reader of tea-leaves and palms, he had imposed his imagination onto the observation and drawn a faulty conclusion based on hopes, wishes, and dreams. On close inspection, his civilization turned out to be fissures, mountains, and craters.

Unlike the reader of tea-leaves who claims to read the future, the astronomer had gathered some new information. His conclusions may have been incorrect, but his efforts had value. Whereas, the cunning fortune-teller with her nose in a teacup, merely fools herself and deceives her dupes, and produces a lot of gibberish. The Verity Scanner had increased people's ability to distinguish between what was knowledge and what was nonsense.

Every day, the astronauts were in radio communication with Kronkite and Sara at ground control. It was almost a ritual, like a son or daughter working out-of-state and calling home to mom and dad.

There was not much to discuss. Starfarer had been so well-engineered that there were no equipment complications as of yet. Where words failed, the meters, thermostats, spectroscopes, and other instruments made their own observations and delivered them in digital mathematical language. Atom took readings as asked, absorbing the information but putting little interpretation on it. Scientists on the ground were eagerly assimilating the data, and organizing it into tables, graphs, and stats.

It was almost like being out at sea with all water and horizon and sky,

43

and not much else to distinguish it. And the silence— what could one say about the silence?

Today, however, the astronauts were excited with the prospect of a close look at their first planet since embarking. Video views were to be telecast simultaneously back to the folks at home so they could share the experience. Leading networks were interrupting their regularly-scheduled programming for the exciting event. It was like waiting for an airplane that you see in the distance. Then it grew gradually larger and took on shape and form. Starfarer was approaching a juncture with the planet's elliptical orbit. They would soon meet at an orbital crossroad.

The planet had a diameter of about 41,000 miles, a little over half the size of their own planet.

"How curious it is," exclaimed Darla, as the four astronauts sat in their launch seats and watched as they approached it.

"Isn't it, though?" Atom agreed. "It has a rotation pretty close to home, but it's orbiting much slower."

"Yeah, it's like a big spaceship without a pilot," said Orwell. "Fascinating, but drab-looking. No clouds, no atmosphere."

This was the first time since departing that Atom would steer Starfarer. Everything that the flight simulator had taught his reflexes was about to be tested. Much would depend on the accuracy of his navigational charting which he had done in his early training.

They would not land on this planet, nor loiter to examine it. They couldn't expend the time or fuel. They had a much more important objective and time was essential. Other scientists in the future might lavish attention on it. It was not Starfarer's mission. Astronomers had pretty much ruled out the planet's value for colonization.

Starfarer's cameras would, however, provide a close and valuable view of the planet. Equally important, it would give Starfarer a gravity assist. Coming within the planet's rotational gravity field would add acceleration to the spaceship. Catapulting it onward on their journey. This borrowed energy would maximize Starfarer's speed and minimize its fuel consumption. It could be dangerous, but accomplished successfully, it was a very good energy deal.

Suddenly, the planet loomed large in their sight. The astronauts were strapped in their pilothouse seats. The planet filled their view like a huge movie screen and they had front row seats.

Perspiration beaded Atom's brow and his palms were moist. "Hold on," he said, "this is it!"

"Let 'er go, daddy-o!" whooped Orwell.

The rocket ship was hurtling towards the monstrous dull-gray craggy globe. The aspect of it before their eyes was ominous compared to the colorful life-rich planet that had been their home.

What they saw beneath them was a desolate rocky terrain. A forbidding angular landscape. One could imagine climbing cliffs and clefts, kicking rocks, hearing them clatter as they tumbled down deep chasms. That is, if there was air to carry sound waves. There was nothing soft to delight the eye or raise the spirit. It was a stone mason's dream, a sculptor's paradise, and a common man's nightmare.

They whizzed by the bleak planet like travelers passing a billboard—curious about its appearance, but also repelled by it. Atom had done his homework. He had set his course with precision. Only a slight finesse of the controls was necessary. Kronkite's value of being thorough paid off.

"Yow-ee! That was a whipper!" exclaimed Orwell.

Atom turned to look at Darla. "You all right?" he asked.

Darla looked a little green. "Yes, I'm okay."

Evelyn put her hand on Darla's arm and smiled.

Kronkite's voice came over the speaker. "Well done, Atom. I couldn't have executed the maneuver better myself. Perhaps not as well."

"Thank you, sir," said Atom.

"Anyone have any impressions they want to share about this encounter?" asked Kronkite.

"Yes, once we catch our breath." said Evelyn. "That planet could benefit from some help from mother nature. It needs water. It needs some wilderness. It needs agriculture. Maybe with some good humus, some seeds and watering, it could be made friendly to farming."

"Yeah," quipped Orwell. "I think it'd be better for a rock garden. That's what I think of it. I don't see much else for it. No real estate agent would list it. Sure would take a lot of convicts to break up all those boulders."

They all laughed.

Back at the base, footage taken by Starfarer's cameras was repeated several times over the air. Although the view was brief and the stony surface offered little picture variety, it attracted wide public attention because of its novelty and exotic location. To the public, the four astronauts became their 'eyes in the sky'. It was even run in slow motion. Still shots were printed in newspapers and magazines.

The astronaut's feat had made them more famous than ever. One columnist coined a name for the crew of Starfarer: 'Atom's apples'.

Later, the scientists would subject the photos of the planet to intensive study, noting its geological formations, and charting its surface.

Days later, after the energy boost, the astronauts returned to their regular routines and the journey continued.

Up to now, joyous and expansive Orwell, practically skipped from duty to duty. He was engrossed in the working of the systems like a child at play. For relaxation and recreations, he spent most his free time viewing sports from back home. Then the television signal began to weaken. He tried various things to enhance it. As television weakened, Orwell seemed to weaken as well. His gait altered. His step slowed. He became sluggish. He seemed to study the floor a lot. Finally, the TV picture faded altogether. No amplification would bring it back.

Darla first noticed the change in his disposition. She could not understand his altered attitude towards her. She desperately tried to comfort him, to no avail. Usually buoyant, he became quiet and taciturn. She kept it to herself. She shouldered the blame for his moodiness, and absorbed his sharp retorts as if she were guilty of some offense.

A new climate entered the confines of Starfarer in the form of Orwell's mood swing.

CHAPTER VIII

Over two months passed. The astronaut couples were settled into their shifts, twelve hours on and twelve hours off. All based on chronometer time, not sunrises and sunsets. There was no welcoming sunshine streaming in the window, no birds singing to greet the day. They all worked on the night-shift of space. Lacking sunrise and sunset, all that differentiated their daily schedule was the clock.

They were millions of miles from governmental control, therefore no regulations could be forced on them, and yet a thread of performance persisted in the form of habit and yes, perhaps the desire to please Kronkite.

Essentially, the only form of normality left them was the schedule they lived by in their former lives. That consisted merely of daily time segments. And all that stood between them and total release from all former constraints, was habit and training, the demand of survival, and their established relationships.

Their needs were very basic, the means for gratifying them extremely technological. They monitored their own atmosphere. They raised and harvested their own food. They provided their own diversions, entertainments, and companionship.

As the wake-up alarm sounded, the newlyweds, Atom and Evelyn, warm under their bed covers, woke. Atom reached over and turned on the light.

"Good morning, sweetheart," Atom said yawning and rubbing his eyes.

Evelyn's head turned on her pillow and she smiled. "Morning," she replied. "I had the strangest dream last night." Out of custom, she called their rest-time 'night' although all around them was always night.

"Oh, what was it about?"

"I dreamt the plants had developed personalities and were fighting to take over the spaceship."

"Oh no, really?"

"Yes, and I was trying to convince them not to do it. But they wouldn't listen to me. They started to organize and everything."

"Oh, my gosh."

"Yes, they were planning a revolution."

47

"Sounds like a grass-root's rebellion. What did you do, attempt to nip it in the bud?"

"Cute, sweetheart. Make fun of my dream, will you?" Playfully she tossed her pillow at him.

"I think you've been talking with your plants too much lately. That's your trouble."

"More than likely, it's something I ate last night that didn't sit well."

"Probably one of your salads talking back," chuckled Atom.

Evelyn slipped out of her nightgown. "It was all so very vivid as I dreamt it. Being out in space somehow makes the unlikely all the more credible."

Atom reached out and pulled her to him in a tight embrace. "I'll tell you one thing I'm certain of," he said. "<u>You</u> are incredible."

"Oh," she sighed. "I'll bet you tell that to all the plant physiologists you know."

Atom laughed. "You're right, I do."

"This feels nice, but it's not getting me dressed."

"I know."

"Besides, Darla and Orwell are going to wonder what's keeping us."

"That's all right. We can say marauding plants detained us."

"Ah, but they might test us with the Verity Scanner, then what?" chided Evelyn.

"You're right. We'd better move it if we're going to get to the dining room on time." Evelyn and Atom left their room together and walked down the hallway to the galley. "I've got to hand it to you, sweetheart, the greenhouse is really working. As vegans, we haven't dipped into our reserves at all. The food's been good and so is our health. I don't know how you do it," said Atom.

"If you're good, I'll let you in on my professional secrets."

"Okay, do you sweet talk the plants into producing or tyrannize them? Tell me that, my little farmerette."

"You sweet-talking traveling salesmen are all alike. You go for the farmer's daughter, don't you?"

Atom laughed.

They entered the dining room compartment. Darla was sitting by the table alone.

"Morning, Darla," greeted Atom.

"It's evening to her, sweetheart," corrected Evelyn.

"Where's Orwell?"

"He ate quickly and left. Said he had to check the air exchanger."

"Oh," said Atom. "Sorry we missed him. Anything the matter? No trouble with the exchanger, I hope."

48

"No, it's okay," said Darla, hardly looking up from her plate. "I'm going to put in some extra time on the ROSS scanner."

"During your free time?" Atom asked. "Have you found a frequency with some promising signals?"

"Not yet. Maybe tonight— sorry I mean morning— I might get lucky." Darla cleared her dishes rather hurriedly and walked to the door.

"Okay." said Atom. "After we eat, I'm coming up to the control room to check the autopilot. I'll see you there."

Darla closed the door and left.

Atom and Evelyn looked at each other inquisitively.

"Um-m," murmured Atom. "What's that all about?"

"I don't know," pondered Evelyn. "Something's bothering her. Isn't it unusual for Orwell not to be here? He usually sticks around for a little chat before he goes off for his recreation time. Do you suppose there's something the matter with the air exchanger?"

"I'll certainly check with him later," said Atom, sitting down to breakfast. "What are you doing this morning?"

"Disciplining the dream plants and keeping them from rebelling," she joked.

They finished their breakfast in relative silence. And then Evelyn turned to head to the greenhouse, while Atom headed left toward the control room.

"If you meet Orwell on the way, ask him to see me if there are any problems."

"Okay, sweetheart."

"And by the way....," he said hesitating...

"Yes?"

"...are you well-armed to defend yourself against your rampaging plants?"

Evelyn laughed. "Don't worry, I can always chew my way through. See you at lunch time?"

"Yeah."

They kissed and parted, smiling.

Darla was sitting at the radio console when Atom entered the control room. She greeted him with a little smile, but didn't say anything. He interpreted her silence to mean she had no radio signals to report. So, he didn't ask her.

Atom went to Starfarer's propulsion controls and checked their course. The surveillance screen was black punctuated with scattered sparkling dots. To the uninformed, they looked like a random scattering— luminous grains of sand on a dark background. A simple person might treat them like dot puzzles and connect the dots with lines and call them animals or whatever imaginary creatures his fancy could invent like shepherds of old had done. Such a person might even invest such dot creatures with magical powers.

For Atom, they were stars, galaxies, planets, and moons. Some so distant that it would take many, many lifetimes to reach them. His hope, and the hope of the Starfarer expedition, was that he could reach one of the nearest planets or moons and find one habitable. It was an awesome responsibility.

There was a remote possibility that one of the outer planets in their own orbital system might prove suitable. But the prognostication was not good. So, they could not afford to spend much time searching before heading on.

For the last few days, Atom charted Starfarer's next planet rendezvous. He hoped to gain the maximum gravity assist from it, and come out aimed for his next destination whatever he determined that to be. The two factors were interdependent. One, to borrow maximum thrust, and two, to steer a true subsequent course.

While working on the navigation, Atom stole a glance at Darla at the ROSS radio console. It was unusual for her to be scanning frequencies during her recreation time. She'd already put in an eight-hour shift. She looked tired. Atom finished his calculations and walked over and stood by her.

"Darla, I know what you're doing is important, but don't you think you've done enough today?"

She looked weary and sad. She had the look that said— 'I'm feeling bad, ask me about it.'

"Tell me. What is it? What's bothering you?"

Darla stood up and threw herself into Atom's arms, sobbing. "Orwell...Orwell doesn't love me anymore. And..and...Oh, I don't know what I'll do."

Atom tried to comfort her. Setting a course, dealing with quadrants, degrees, trajectories, that was one thing. But this? He was totally ill-prepared to cope with it. He held her close and tried to collect his thoughts.

"Why, what gives you that idea? What happened? Did you two have an argument, or..."

"... No. He's just grown cold. He doesn't talk— I don't know why— he hardly... hardly notices me. Oh, what'll I do?" she sobbed some more.

Atom felt terrible for her, but helpless. Marriage counseling was just not in his repertoire.

They stood for some time in the embrace. Atom lightly patted her shoulder. While standing, they didn't notice the control room door open. Orwell was about to enter. When he saw Darla in Atom's arms, he stopped, took a long look, and then slowly backed out the door and quietly closed it.

Atom and Darla were unaware Orwell had seen them together.

Finally, Atom said, "Look, it's time for a break. Let's go see Evelyn. What d'ya say?"

Darla nodded and brushed away a tear from her cheek.

As they walked down the passageway, Orwell saw them pass by. He was watching from the shadows where he was hiding.

Atom and Darla entered the dining room and found Evelyn back from the greenhouse.

"Look," said Evelyn, "our first fruit!" She held the golden-orange fruit in her cupped hands. "Try some. Go ahead, try some." She bubbled with glee and pride.

Atom and Darla tasted the shiny fruit. As Atom bit through the peel, juice trickled into his mouth and down his chin.

"How's it taste?" asked Evelyn beaming.

"Hmm-m-mm, good, sweetheart, fantastic," said Atom, wiping a drop of juice from the corner of his mouth."

"Oh, I'm so excited!" said Evelyn. "The growing light mix is effective. The bees are working. Everything's growing!"

Atom thought of Darla's problem, but he couldn't think how to bring it up now without dampening Evelyn's joy. He decided to discuss the problem later with Evelyn, when they were alone.

"By the way, did you see Orwell when you were coming from the greenhouse? He would have gone through there if he was checking the air supply."

"No," said Evelyn. "I haven't seen him once all day long. Haven't you?"

Just then the door opened and Orwell burst in.

"C'mon," he said to Darla, grabbing her roughly by the arm. "It's time to go to bed."

He abruptly left the dining room with Darla in tow, slamming the door, and leaving Evelyn and Atom in shock and consternation at his behavior.

CHAPTER IX

Darla and Orwell had disappeared into their quarters, leaving Atom and Evelyn to wonder at the scene which had just taken place.

"What was that all about? Do you know?" asked Evelyn.

Atom could only shake his head and ponder.

"I've noticed that Orwell has been unusually moody lately," she added, "but that's the first time I've seen him act so erratically. What do you suppose is the matter?"

"It has affected Darla as well," said Atom. "She broke down in the control room and said that she felt Orwell doesn't love her anymore. Maybe you could have a talk with her and get to the bottom of it. I'm at a loss to know what to do."

"I'll do what I can," said Evelyn. "In the meantime, at least we can lend her a sympathetic ear till this rift blows over. I don't think any interference on our part would be wise at this time."

"Yes," said Atom, "I think you're right. He just may be out of sorts and time will handle it. Do you think I should mention it to Sara or Kronkite? I'll be talking with them on their afternoon visit."

"No, I don't think I would mention it, if I were you. What purpose would it serve? It would just worry them unnecessarily with a problem that's not really their concern. And besides, what could they do about it anyway?"

"It would have to happen now. Especially with my next planet intersect coming up."

"Oh, how soon will that be?"

"In twenty-four days from now, as near as I can estimate. So, you see, I have a lot on my mind."

"Of course." Evelyn put her hand on his arm.

"The fruit was delicious, sweetheart," said Atom. "Do you need any help in the greenhouse this afternoon?"

"No, not today. You go do what you have to do. I'll see you at lunch."

Atom and Evelyn had a quiet lunch and an uneventful space afternoon of work. They had no expectation of seeing Orwell or Darla at this hour, for it was the couple's hour swing-shift and they would undoubtedly be sleeping.

Finally, it was Atom and Evelyn's dinner-time, and breakfast-time for Orwell and Darla.

Atom and Evelyn sat down at the dining room table. The dishes were set as usual. The meal was typical. Everything in the room was in place. All was ordinary, and yet there was a singularity about it. Picking up a fork and knife and eating was different. The dining room atmosphere was charged with some pervasive mood. There was an inexplicable tension which the dropping of a pin could have set off. That, or the appearance of Orwell.

The ominous silence was at last broken by the galley door opening.

Darla entered.

"Good morning, Darla," said Evelyn.

"Morning," replied Darla, somewhat sheepishly. She began busily making breakfast.

Atom and Evelyn continued eating. They gave each other searching glances. Neither could think of anything fitting to say. Perhaps when they all sat at the table, as they usually did, the ice would be broken, and normal conversation resume.

In the galley, the usually talkative Darla quietly continued her breakfast preparations, careful not to break the oppressive silence. When finished, Darla put everything on a tray.

"I hope you'll forgive us," she said very meekly. "We're going to have breakfast in our room." So saying, Darla turned and left.

Evelyn and Atom looked at each other, mystified. "Now, what do you make of that?"

"I don't know what to make of it," said Atom. "I might expect such a breakfast of newlyweds like us— but let's not jump to any conclusions. It may be that we're reading more into it than the circumstances justify."

"Let's get our minds off it," said Evelyn. "It's our recreation time."

"You're right," said Atom getting up from the table. "We can damn well use some relaxation. Before that, though, I've got to make one last check of our bearings up in the control room. Do you want to come with me?"

"I have a few things to put away first, and then I'll join you," she answered.

He leaned over and kissed Evelyn before leaving the room.

As Atom walked down the passageway toward the control room, he thought what it would be like to encounter Orwell. The day's events were certainly casting a pall over everything. He was reminded how it felt walking down the street back home and meeting up with a hostile unfriendly neighbor. How chilly the effect of it was.

Orwell was on his work-shift now. That could take him anywhere in the spaceship. Atom went   to the computer/data room and then into the control room. It was empty, and for once, Atom was glad.

He looked at the surveillance screen. Starfarer was still hurtling through the dark infinite reaches of space. Gravity was such a compelling factor back home, but out in this void it was negligible. Without their propelling rockets, they would float and drift endlessly, like a speck of dust on a thermal updraft, not knowing up from down. On minimum energy, they sped along on perpetual overdrive. They had no way of knowing, once launched, what forces they might encounter. Most of the best scientific minds presumed more space, more space and more space.

*   *   *

Sara and Kronkite entered the glassed-in communication's room. Sara had persuaded her husband to take the day off and go for a picnic at Rainbow Lake. For a man who loved his work as much as Kronkite did, pulling him away from the Space Center, was like wresting honey from a grizzly bear. You couldn't expect to do it without a fight or a snarl.

"Kronkite, calling Starfarer. Are you receiving me? Over." He turned to Sara. "This is Atom's time off."

"Probably nobody's in the control room."

"Try again, dear," urged Sara." Darla's apt to be at the radio console."

"Kronkite calling Starfarer."

For ten seconds, the speaker hissed dead silence. Then a voice sounded. "This is Starfarer."

"Atom, this is Kronkite. Glad I reached you. Sara talked me into a picnic today. That's why I'm not calling at the regular time. Over."

"She did, did she? Good for her. Is Sara there with you now? Over."

"Yes, I'm here Atom. How are you and Evelyn? Over."

"Fine. She's fine, too. Not in the control room at the moment, however, or I'd put her on. Going on a picnic, hey? I'd forgotten— summer has come for you. Where are you going on your picnic? Over."

"Rainbow Lake. Wish you two could be with us. Over"

"Me too. I'm afraid it's a bit too far for us to drive," Atom laughed, somewhat ironically. "Rainbow is a nice lake. I used to go swimming there as a kid. Are you going in? Over."

"I am," said Sara, "but I don't think I can talk Kronkite into it. The only way to get him in the water would be in diving gear where there was something he wanted to see on the bottom. You know his insatiable curiosity. Over."

"You're right. Next thing you'd know, he'd be planning to colonize the sea bottom. Over."

Sara arched her eyebrows and looked at Kronkite. They smiled at each other.

"Don't you go giving him any new ideas, Atom," said Sara. "He still owes me that vacation he promised me. Over."

"Well, don't let him off the hook, Sara. Use me for a witness of his promise, if you like. Over."

"Thanks, I will...."

"No conspiracies, you two," interjected Kronkite. "Has Darla picked up any signals over her ROSS scanner? Over."

"Not yet. She's been diligent at it, too. Oh, and by the way, Sara, keep after that husband of yours. Notice how he quickly changes the subject? Don't let him talk you out of the picnic. Over."

"Thanks, I won't. I'm quite familiar with his techniques," laughed Sara.

"That's for sure," joined in Kronkite, smiling. "A psychologist for a wife makes a tough taskmaster. She knows every rationalization in the book. But tell me, Atom, how are Orwell and Darla? Still as chipper as ever, I hope. Over."

"Yes, everything's... pretty routine. Over."

"That's good," said Kronkite. "Anything else to report? Over."

"No. That's about it. You and Sara have a good picnic. Skip a stone in the lake for me. Over."

"I'll do that. Take care. Over and out."

Sara and Kronkite left the control center and walked to their car in the parking lot. When they were seated in the car, Sara turned to Kronkite and asked. "Okay, what is it?"

"What's what?" he asked.

"I can read your face like a book, you know. Something's bothering you."

"You're right. Something is bothering me," said Kronkite, looking down as if he was chasing some vagrant thought. "You know when I asked about Orwell and Darla? Well, I had the Verity Scanner turned on." He turned and looked at Sara. "Atom didn't tell me the truth."

CHAPTER X

As Sara and Kronkite drove over the crest of the hill, Rainbow Lake came into view. It was a magnificent sight. The water gleaming as it did in the sunshine— its sparkling shimmering surface reflected the deep blue sky and billowing clouds. Summer freshness was everywhere warming, wafting, and flowering.

Parking the car, they stepped around back and opened the trunk to get their picnic basket, blanket, and beach umbrella. Sara peered out from under her large-brimmed hat as Kronkite pulled on his visor tightening his cap by a tug, against the lake breeze.

They sauntered side by side to the shore. Waves lightly lapped and receded leaving flecks of foam that seeped into the sand. "How about here?" suggested Sara.

Kronkite carefully set down the picnic basket. Its handle dropped with a tiny clink.

Sara unfolded their beach blanket. Held by the corners, they gave it a snap so it settled lightly on a cushion of air down onto the sand.

"What a perfect day to be here." Sara stretched out her arms. "A person must be really impoverished, who never takes one minute to enjoy a day like this," she said.

They sat down facing the lake, their arms clasped around their knees tucked up under their chins. Sara then kicked off her sandals and wiggled her toes in the sand's warmth.

"I have to admit, darling. With all my quests, I too often neglect taking time to enjoy life."

"That's a great admission on your part," assented Sara.

"It makes you wonder, doesn't it, why anyone would cloud their mind with drugs, when such glorious beauty as this is free to delight the senses."

"After years of clinical study, I can only conclude that they must be desperately unhappy, mentally ill, or stupid to sacrifice good health in trade for a chemical delusion.

"It is a shame. Life is too precious to squander or waste," agreed Kronkite.

"Isn't it odd," said Sara, "that all that is really priceless, is truly without a price? If only people would realize it. As the saying goes: 'the best things in life are free'— like joy, friendship, and love."

"Hmm-mm," mused Kronkite. "Joy, friendship, and love." He rolled the idea slowly over in his mind. "You're right. Of course, a lot of time is spent pursuing those."

"Yes, and that's the paradox. You can't seek them. You can only get them by giving them. There's no other way. It's profoundly simple, as I see it," summarized Sara. "It's an exchange— a gift for a gift."

Sara and Kronkite gazed out at the quiescent lake with the summer breeze rippling over its surface.

"You know, one thing I don't understand. Most creatures seem to have the survival instinct. They fight when cornered, flee from danger whenever possible. They seek shelter. Often, they band together for safety. Yet, of our own kind, there are those who bemoan life, seek escape, and destroy themselves. It seems to defy the survival instinct. I don't know that suicide exists in any other species. We can't talk to the animals to find that out, of course. I wonder what we might learn if we could master their language? Now that's a subject I could see pursuing."

"There you go again," smiled Sara, as she opened the lid of the picnic basket, "endlessly pursuing!" She handed him an egg-salad sandwich.

They savored their lunch and enjoyed the Rainbow Lake scenery. Gazing at the sky, they watched the sun drift slowly toward the horizon. Finished with lunch, they strolled along the shore.

"The more I think of it," said Kronkite, "it must be a part of the whole survival instinct that our species keeps moving on. What else could it be? Such restlessness. Some species are limited to one corner of the globe. Another becomes extinct altogether. But we keep adapting, keep migrating. Maybe that's what's impelling the Starfarer project. It could be, you know. Sometimes it seems to me to be mere curiosity. Or maybe it's the desire for adventure. Or perhaps fame. Or perhaps to make history. Then again, underlying it all, perhaps unconsciously is the survival instinct at work."

Sara stopped and picked up a wonderfully gnarled piece of driftwood. All its roughness worn away by rolling in the surf. It was marbled and smooth to the touch. Many seasons had shaped the driftwood into a design of some sensuous beauty. It had withstood the rough wear and not disintegrated.

"I marvel when I think how Starfarer may be a whole new evolutionary start," said Kronkite. They came to a halt at a tree that over-hung the lake shore. The tree's roots tenaciously gripped the bank against infiltration of the waves. "Of course, all starts are endings and beginnings."

"I just hope our colonizing astronauts don't fall victim to the war, greed, and superstition that our ancestors endured before the Verity Scanner exposed the perpetrators of those crimes."

"If we have, I imagine, in recounting it, you'll be glorified as a mythic god figure, heroic in aspect and demeanor," said Sara, leaning against the tree trunk and gazing dreamily at the sunset.

"I hope not!" declared Kronkite emphatically breaking the spell. "That would be deplorable. It would falsify all I've worked for, the freedom I've stood for my whole life. It would be like going back to primitive times. Back to being ruled by madmen who craved, above all else, riches and adulation. Those narcissists who dress up in silly hats and costumes, who are fond of flags, banners, badges, and conquest, and secretly despise people. Those evil ones who over the centuries have caused unspeakable atrocities, mayhem, and misery. Their one goal, throughout history, has been to selfishly destroy freedom and force humanity into submission to their rapacious will."

"I well know your passion, darling," said Sara. "The past that was, is undeniable. Is it the astronaut's future that most worries you? Or are you feeling responsible for what may happen to them?"

"Of course, you're right," said Kronkite. "Pardon me for going off on one of my rants. I do worry about them, though."

"Don't take all the responsibility on yourself, dear. Everyone was aware of the risks inherent in the project. Risk taking is one of the attributes of our species. No pain, no gain."

"Easily said."

"Then what worries you most?"

"Most?" Kronkite stroked his wrinkled chin. "I think it's their extreme youth. Wisdom isn't gained without years of experience, and even then, sometimes not. Life doesn't allow much time to acquire wisdom before the book is closed. If only I could have gone with them. That I regret."

"So far, I haven't detected any regret on their part. They seem resolute enough, although their existence cooped up in that spacecraft must be terrible. Chance will be a very big factor. If fortune is not on their side, they're in a situation with no escape."

Sara took hold of her husband's arm as they headed back to their beach blanket.

As they walked, Kronkite took the moment to reflect: "I'm satisfied we selected them well— good personalities, genetic makeup, training, skills, potential for growth. Of course, I do worry how it will end for them. I'm concerned about their judgment. It has taken a long time for reason to evolve. I've been thinking of concepts which would be a capsule of all I have learned over a lifetime." Kronkite's face became animated as he spoke.

"Many of the early societies were created by prophets who claimed to receive rules from some mysterious authority in a voice only the prophet could hear. These prophets claimed high ideals but invariably distrusted reason, and demanded from their subject's unquestioned obedience. Punishment, torture, and war were their weapons. They were the kings and emperors who ruled by so-called divine right and made themselves gods. I would not want to be party to any of their schemes."

"The only system is one that guarantees absolute freedom. One that can face the scrutiny of the Verity Scanner without flinching. For that, I would like to suggest a code. One that could be based on the best accumulated knowledge. A code for all. Leaders especially, would have to adhere to it. In the past, bad leaders have caused more widespread misery than any individual could on his own."

"It would be a code that the astronauts could take with them. Perhaps into a new planetary home."

"Sounds like an exciting idea," said Sara who always had an ear for Kronkite's restless mind.

Kronkite stopped, faced Sara, and looked into his wife's eyes. "If I attempt such a code, would you help me with it? I would want it to be equally fair to both men and women, not biased against women like the old creeds have been. I'd want your input."

They arrived back at their beach blanket. The shadow from their beach umbrella now stretched with the setting sun. Everything had taken on a reddish-orange hue. They gathered their blanket, shook off the sand, and folded it.

Kronkite picked up a smooth flat stone, and walked to the lake's edge. Side-armed, he threw the stone and watched it skip— four, five, six times over the surface of the lake. "That's for Atom," he said. Sara and Kronkite returned to their car and drove off. They were invigorated by the lake air and their stroll on the beach. The landscape vibrated with warmth. A riot of fragrance swirled through the car vents from the verdant fields.

Sara was quiet. Atom was on her mind. What had triggered the Verity Scanner's response? She suspected it was on Kronkite's mind, also. Especially since he had avoided discussing it. He was always keen on details, and like a perky fox terrier, worried over them till he tracked down the source of his unease. Sara decided to broach the subject with him.

"You're concerned about your talk with Atom this morning, aren't you?"

"Yes and... no," said Kronkite. "I know I'm being vague, but that's how I feel. Yes, I was surprised. It was unexpected. But perhaps it's only a minor problem. It may even be insignificant. In any case, I didn't want it to spoil our day at the beach or our picnic."

He smiled at Sara and they drove on enjoying the pleasure of the ride in the country. Always involved in operations at the center, he seldom

59

delegated decision-making authority, or responsibility. This was one of those rare times Kronkite had taken a day off. He had enjoyed it and it did relax him, partially. It was a form of token payment for another real debt he had incurred. That was the vacation he had promised Sara and as yet not fulfilled. Kronkite did not like breaking a promise.

CHAPTER XI

A person never has enough responsibility until he's handed more. At least that was the way it seemed to Atom. What was the saying? If you want to get something done, hand it to a busy person.

Atom felt overloaded. He felt mentally and physically drained. It affected his sleep. He rolled one way, then the other. His brain felt charged with electric energy. There was a ringing in one ear. His eyes felt gummy. With all his restlessness, he tried to avoid waking Evelyn. Perhaps sex could give him some release from tension, but he was far from being in an amorous mood, and he didn't want to disturb Evelyn's rest. No use both of them losing sleep.

He tried different sleeping positions. Arms under the covers. Arms out of the covers. Bunch up his pillow. Turn to his other side. Think meditation. Try different breathing techniques. Imagine a sunny day on an exotic island. Curl up in a fetal position. Stare into the darkness. Get out of bed and go to the privy. Yawn. Stretch. Think over what was bothering him.

Yes, what was bothering him? That was probably it. Resolve some difficulties in his mind and they would go away so he could rest.

What were the difficulties?

The entire Starfarer project, for one. It was a major undertaking and irreversible. At least not   without good reason. It wasn't like being a truck driver and driving a route, and then parking and taking a day off. No, days off on a spaceship? It didn't work that way. You stayed with this cargo. This truck never stopped rolling.

And that was another thing. This project was a long tour. You didn't sign on for two years and have the option to re-enlist. That wasn't the way it worked. Once signed on and aboard, you were committed to the end of the journey. And the end was uncertain because the destination was unknown. Did he have what it takes to see it through and not crack? There was no escape from the stress of it.

Then there was the next planet intersect coming up— as near as he could figure— in about four months. Months! As if months had any relevance to the cosmos. Changes are always unsettling. Always the question and the doubt whether one has made the right decision. He had

61

decided to skip the very next planetary orbit and go for the largest planet in the galaxy. His thinking was a little like a driver on a turnpike— the fewer stops the better the time. But that wasn't necessarily the case in space travel. With a sling-shot gravity assist, he actually gained speed if executed properly. The maneuver was not without tension and danger, and another source of restlessness. When he climbed into bed he had left the control room behind him, but the piloting of Starfarer climbed in bed with him. His navigational duties were always on his mind, lurking somewhere.

Then there was Starfarer itself. A massive piece of equipment. It was as vulnerable as any vehicle. No sending this back to the shop for repair. No guarantees. No exchanges. Ride it, and repair it. If a part breaks, fix it.

In this, being in space had an advantage. Gravity back home was a great wrecker. It tugged and pulled. It added friction and stress, grinding and wearing out parts. Space was gentler. More gentle than an air-cushioned ride, though air is abrasive to a spaceship traveling at lightening speeds. Air is not everywhere in space. Nothing is as easy on mechanical parts as the nothingness of space.

Electronics were excluded from the advantage of weightlessness. Electrical current performs in its own weightless environment subject to interference from cosmic rays. It was susceptible to problem equally in space as back home. Electronics was Orwell's specialty and responsibility.

Orwell. Another worry. Atom had seen him only briefly down a hallway. He was purposely being shunned by him. It was becoming a psychological nightmare of avoidance. The situation would be difficult enough in a work-place, in the narrow confines of Starfarer, it was hell.

The alarm rang. Atom turned on the light. He felt he hadn't had a wink of sleep. His eyes were heavy, his body leaden. He sat slumped on the edge of the bed. Evelyn woke, turned, and looked at him with concern.

"Good morning," she said. "You sleep well?"

"No, I couldn't sleep at all. Seems like I tossed and turned all night long. I hope I didn't disturb you. I hope I didn't keep you awake."

"Not that I know of. I slept right through."

"Aren't you feeling well?" she asked.

"Too many things on my mind, I think," said Atom. "Couldn't seem to turn off my brain and fall asleep."

"Do you want to stay in bed longer? I could check the bearings and report them back to you."

Evelyn slipped out of her nightgown and began dressing.

"I hadn't better take the time off. Thanks anyway. I don't think another hour in bed would help. I might as well get up and get moving." said Atom, beginning to dress.

Atom yawned lazily, and blinked his eyes as he pulled on his trousers.

A breakfast under his belt, he thought, and he'd feel better.

Atom and Evelyn left their room together and walked down the hallway and entered the galley. They prepared their breakfast and carried it into the dining room and sat down.

"I don't know whether it's tougher not to sleep or to be half awake? I feel half asleep." said Atom. "I think at this point, I'd rather be fully awake. At least then I'd know I wasn't dreaming. By the way, how are your plants doing? Have you managed to subdue their riotous behavior in your dreams?"

"I must have," laughed Evelyn. "I haven't dreamt of them since. So, you see, they're behaving themselves very well. I'm getting good cooperation from them. I guess we're safe at present time from any attack of the warring plants."

"People should be as docile," said Atom.

"Plants aren't as peace-loving as you think. They're in competition, too. They fight for light, and ground space, and nourishment, and a place to root and spread, just as their animal brethren do. Also, they travel and establish new colonies. They just compete at a slower, less noticeable speed."

"Wow, I hadn't thought about that. Of course, there are weeds. They have to be the most aggressive scurrilous warring plants of all," said Atom.

"Not really. That's unjustly imposing our prejudice on them. A weed is a plant we haven't found a use for as yet. It's not fair to condemn them on that account. They have as much right to existence as anything. Many weeds are more resourceful than domesticated plants. One must give them credit. Compared to domestics, weeds survive on their own with little assistance. They're truly free, independent, and self-sufficient."

"Three cheers for the weeds!" said Atom.

At just that instant, Orwell and Darla entered.

"Who is being toasted?" asked Orwell, with a catlike grin. "Did you say weeds?"

Orwell and Darla walked over to the table and sat down. They sat down like the clock had been turned back, and nothing had intervened in the meantime.

"I've never heard of weeds being cheered before." Orwell was his old flippant self again.

"I was just saying, weeds get a bum rap because we haven't found a use for them yet," said Evelyn. "All food plants were, in a sense, weeds once. A worthy project for me as a plant physiologist would be to make food plants as hardy and self-sufficient as weeds. That way we could lessen the work in farming, and conquer the threat of hunger and starvation once and for all."

"Sounds like another job for Kronkite," joked Orwell.

Darla laughed lightly in unison with him.

"Speaking of hungry, honey...," Orwell said, turning to Darla.

"I'll get some dinner," she said, standing up and walking toward the galley.

The conversation, as light as it was, went gaily on. No explanation. No reference to any problem. No hint of complaint. No mention of anything unusual about the previous days. No apologies. It was as if the intervening days of isolation were forgotten, didn't happen, never existed.

After they finished eating together, Evelyn accompanied Atom up to the control room while Orwell and Darla went to the recreation room to watch a movie. Atom checked to be sure the door was shut tight. Then they looked at each other in pure amazement.

"Must be Orwell is over his little snit," said Atom.

"I was just dumbfounded. He came in, sat down, not a word of the last few days. I couldn't believe my ears," said Evelyn.

"Whatever the explanation might be, I'm glad it's over. I hope that's the end of it. You never got one clue about it from Darla, either, did you?"

"Not so much as a hint. Although the subject clearly made her uncomfortable. Darla didn't pursue it, so neither did I."

"Well, it's over, apparently, and I'm glad," said Atom. He walked over to the navigation controls and looked at the surveillance screen.

"Look. See where I'm pointing? That's the third orbiting planet from home. It's very gaseous and extremely cold. The next planet after that isn't in view yet. But we'll intersect with it in ninety-five days or thereabouts. Although it's not habitable, it will give us a tremendous boost."

"What comes after that?" said Evelyn, studying the screen.

"Our final planet," continued Atom, "you can barely see it. It's so far out, not much is known about it. It may be habitable, for all we know. Or perhaps have a moon that would be. That's our last chance to stay in our own planetary system."

"What are the odds we'll find a livable one?"

"Not good," said Atom, shaking his head. "And we can't land to consider our options, you know. Our trip would be over. We don't have the capacity to relaunch again."

"What then?"

"The best we can hope for, when we reach the outermost planet, is a better view of the stars to head for. At that point, we'll have to decide which galaxy to target. That will be a big decision to make. The distance will be so great, greater than any we've plied so far, I dread even to think about it."

Evelyn was very close to Atom. She put her arm about him. "Has anyone ever taken such a long honeymoon trip as us?" she smiled giving him a little kiss.

Just then, the radio console loudspeaker began a static hiss.

"Mm-mm," said Evelyn. "I didn't know we radiated that much electricity, sweetheart."

The speaker hissed some more. It was Kronkite.

"Kronkite calling Starfarer. Are you receiving me?"

Atom and Evelyn walked over to the radio console and clicked the switch. "This is Starfarer, Evelyn and Atom here. Go ahead. Over."

"Evelyn is there too? Fine. How is the greenhouse doing? Over."

"Quite well, thanks. The plants are good passengers really. They seem to thrive with the motion. I call it the cradle effect. After centuries of being immobile and root-bound, they are getting to move about and they seem to respond to it. I've experimented with various intervals and I find that we can augment our food production. At home, you're stuck with your seasons, while here I control all those factors. Unless you can do something about the spin and orbit of your world, you'll never be able to match my production. Over."

"Sounds like you're having good success. What about any of the weightless experiments you're trying? Over."

"That's been interesting, too. The plant stems and branches are amazed to find they're free from all that weight-bearing. It's rather comical to see the fruit floating about like a halo. I'm not sure it has any practical applications, yet, but it is novel and aesthetically pleasing to see. If I had enough space to grow an apple tree, picking the apples would be easy. I could simply float over and pick the topmost apples without a ladder. Over."

"I'll make a note of that, Evelyn," said Kronkite, "and design a larger spaceship just for an orchard. Over"

"Evelyn's making a note of it, too, sir. She'll be sending a requisition for it as soon as you establish intergalactic mail service. Over."

"Postal service? Delivery would be difficult. Ha, ha! How are things with you, Atom? By the way, Orwell and Darla, how are they doing?"

Atom and Evelyn's eyes met quickly, seeking an appropriate reply. "Mm-m okay, so far as we know. You'd have to ask them. They perform their duties well. No complaint there. How was your picnic at Rainbow Lake with Sara? Over."

"Very pleasant. It took some of the heat off me for delaying Sara's vacation. Incidentally, I skipped that stone for you— it skipped six times," said Kronkite, adding: "Can't you tell me anything more about Darla and Orwell? Over."

"Don't see much of them being on swing-shifts. Just finished eating together. Learned about weeds from Evelyn. Over.'"

"Are you sure there's not more to say about Orwell and Darla?" asked Sara, who had just arrived at the center and joined the conversation.

"Hello, Sara. This is Evelyn. Nice to hear your voice. Is there something you know and we don't about Darla and Orwell? Have you talked to them recently? Over."

"Yes, we have talked to Darla. She was not very communicative. Not her usual up self. That's why I was hoping you could shed some more light on it," said Sara. "Over."

"Is that why you were pressing me on it?" asked Atom. "We also were puzzled by their behavior. Especially Orwell's. Today at mealtime, they were back to their ordinary selves. That's as much as we know. Orwell just acted strangely for a few days. We're hoping it's all blown over, whatever their problem was. Over."

"Thanks, Atom. As long as you don't think anything is seriously wrong, I won't worry about it. If any problems *do* arise, no matter how minor, please don't hesitate to confer with us. Okay? Over."

"Thanks, sir. We appreciate the advice you and Sara give us. Have a nice day. Over."

"Thanks to you both. Goodbye for now. Over and out."

Atom switched the radio back onto standby.

"That was very astute of Kronkite and Sara to pick up on Orwell's odd behavior from millions of miles away, wasn't it?" said Atom. "Do you think he knows something we don't?"

"That's hard to say, I don't know any reason he would keep it from us, do you?"

A slight frown played across Evelyn's face. "It's all very mysterious, isn't it? It would seem Orwell's behavior would fall more into Sara's department."

"Right. As much as Kronkite is a stickler for the smallest detail, I'm sure he would consult Sara. This is really a dilemma for me, in a way," said Atom.

"Why?"

"On the one hand, we could have shared a little more information with them. On the other hand, should we? Isn't it an invasion of Darla and Orwell's privacy?"

"Let's hope it's over and done with. I've got some work to do in the greenhouse. Want to help me?"

"Sure," said Atom. "Lead on, sweet Mother Nature."

CHAPTER XII

The next day after Kronkite and Sara had radioed Starfarer and talked with Atom and Evelyn, Sara drove up to the center to pick up her hard-working husband.

He was sitting in his high-backed chair pivoted around away from his desk facing the window.

"Dear, I'm starved. Will you take me out to dinner? Oh, I'm sorry." she said. "I didn't mean to break your train of thought."

"No harm done. I'm glad you came to get me. My engine could use some refueling. Before we go, can you think of any reason why Orwell has been acting so strangely? Something just doesn't gibe. Would you pull up the CHARM Personality Test file on the astronauts? I wonder if we overlooked something; perhaps some flaw we missed."

Sara pulled up the personality file and printed a copy and handed it to Kronkite. He folded it and placed it in his coat pocket, and they walked out to their car.

A summer rain had washed everything. It was late afternoon, and the rain droplets clinging to the trees glistened like diamonds. The puddled pavement reflected the scene in brilliant wavering colors, as if painted by an artist.

They drove to their favorite restaurant and were seated at a private little table in a white-and-gold curtained alcove.

Kronkite opened the printout and put it next to his bread plate. He drank from his wine glass almost without thinking, his eyes skimming across the CHARM QUOTA test results.

"I don't see anything here that might explain what's going on among the astronauts, or indeed what to look for," said Kronkite. "Interpret the results again for me, as you see them." He handed the unfolded page across to Sara.

"All right," she said putting on her glasses. "I'll start with Atom and Evelyn, and finish with Orwell and Darla."

"Is it necessary to go through all of them?" asked Kronkite.

"It may be, if we're to consider the group dynamic."

Kronkite knew better than to interfere with Sara's methodology.

"I'll look at Atom's results first. In the past performance part of his test,

67

he scored very high in good character. As for honesty, all the astronauts scored extremely high, as was validated by the Verity Scanner. Atom was not a high achiever, but he was an extremely tenacious one. He didn't seem to benefit from much chance good fortune— the throw of the dice, so to speak. Losing both his parents at a very young age is an example of that. It affected his development very much."

"He scored above average in reasoning ability and civility. But he is somewhat indecisive. He's prudent, tempered by courage. He's not apt to act impetuously. He is very balanced between tenacity and accommodation. As you remember, Jordon, the other candidate who was nearly chosen, was superior to Atom in decisiveness, and about equal in the other categories. However, Jordon's spouse did not score anywhere near as strong as Evelyn.

"Yes," smiled Kronkite. "I'm well aware of the value of a nurturing and dynamic helpmate. Didn't I make the best selection in all the world?"

Sara blushed slightly and smiled back. "Flattery always gets you everything. What you don't know is that I was the one who did the selecting."

"Your seductiveness was, and still is, unequaled. Say what they may, a brainy woman is still the best partner in life and in bed, if the guy is man enough to have her," said Kronkite. "An apt comparison is you and Evelyn."

"I noticed how you eyed her, Kronkite."

"Like you, Sara, she is a veritable super woman."

"I would say so, yes," agreed Sara with a grin.

"All that, and a skilled horticulturist, too. That's a pretty unbeatable combination. Of course, a gal trained in psychology is no slouch either. Evelyn did give me an idea, though, in our last space conference."

"A decent one, I hope. What was it?"

"As parking lots and shopping malls use up our good arable land, there may be a need for floating greenhouses someday."

At that point, their waiter served their soup and they took time to eat. When they finished, Sara blotted her mouth with her napkin. The waiter returned. He was a young man, very slender with a sunny disposition.

"How did you like the soup? It's one of our chef's specialties."

"It was very tasty," Sara responded.

The young waiter smiled. "I've been following Starfarer's progress. Do you hear from the astronauts often?"

"Yes... Daily, when radio transmission is possible." said Kronkite.

"It must be difficult living so confined. How are they doing?"

"Fine, just fine," said Kronkite.

"That's good. Glad to hear it." The waiter collected the soup dishes and returned to the kitchen.

"Good thing he wasn't holding a pocket Verity Scanner," said Sara after the waiter had left.

Kronkite blushed a bit. "I know. I fudged a bit, didn't I."

"Yes," grinned Sara, "I'd say you did. Shall I go on with the personality files?"

Kronkite nodded. "Let's skip ahead to Orwell. See if we can figure out what problem he may be having. Let's look at his file."

"All right," Sara said, picking up the file. "Orwell, like the others scored very high in intelligence and knowledge. His past performance was high in achievement. His past contained some prankish behavior, much of it attributed to his extreme youth at the time. He had very doting parents. With his intelligence, he easily manipulated them to serve his wants. However, they were willing participants in the relationship on their own, all to abet his achievement. He's somewhat lower in optimism and not as accommodating in relationships. He had very little family feeling."

"How would Darla figure into his behavior?" asked Kronkite.

"Darla's profile indicates she tends to be a follower, tends to leave the reasoning to others, and is a little risk-averse and fearful. Strong in accommodation, medium in optimism. There you have it all in a computer chip," said Sara.

The light coming through the curtained windows was fading to dusk, so the young waiter lit the little lamp on their table, and then after serving their main entree, returned to the kitchen. Sara and Kronkite enjoyed their dinners. Sara probably tasted more of her dinner than Kronkite, since he kept mulling over the astronauts more than the food.

Leaving the restaurant, they walked out to the parking lot greeted by a chorus of frogs and peepers croaking in a nearby pond. The woods were now cloaked in darkness and only lit by moonlight. A refreshing breeze fanned their faces as they drove home.

After they arrived, parked their car, and entered their home, Kronkite asked, "Now that you have reviewed the test results, what do they suggest to you?"

"One thing occurs to me. Although Atom's prefrontal cortex was more mature than Orwell's, the biggest factor in their choice, after all, was their youth. Evelyn's brain showed the most maturity of the four. However, there is one factor that, no matter how careful our analysis, defies prediction."

"And that is...?"

"Maturity. They're not fully mature yet. Wisdom comes with experience. Experience, of course, is never predictable, and in the case of the astronauts, almost totally unpredictable. Their circumstances and environment are so out of the ordinary. How they mature in space, is anyone's guess."

Kronkite's face wore a thoughtful frown as Sara finished her comment.

"Accept it. We made the best choices possible based on the information we had. Beyond that, it's out of our control. No one can control the future. It's not reasonable to think anyone can. The variety of motives and forces is almost incomprehensible."

"I know that," protested Kronkite.

"I know you do, dear. I know you very well. You tend to take responsibility on yourself, more than any one person should have to bear. Then if the outcome is not as you expect, you blame yourself. That's all right when you're dealing with material that can be tested for failure points. Materials don't have wills of their own like people. With people, some adversity is always to be expected. People will and do disappoint us."

"Now that you've given me your regular college lecture course, I suppose you're going to charge me full tuition?" snickered Kronkite.

"No, sweetheart. I'll accept that wonderful dinner in lieu of payment. Sorry if I sound like I'm lecturing. It's just that you worry too much. More than you should," said Sara.

"Yes, too much," agreed Kronkite. "We'll get some more answers tomorrow. In the meantime, let's go to bed. I'm a lucky guy. I get to sleep with my professor."

CHAPTER XIII

The foremost thought on Atom's mind was progress and speed. He was planning his next planet intersect. He steered a course and mapped it at the same time. As a first-time traveler in space, he set his coordinates as best he could with no landmarks to guide him. Starfarer was hurtling through a whirligig cosmos of shooting, spinning, orbiting, exploding, pulsating starstuff. It was as if the spaceship swam amoeba-like in an airy broth, with sprinkles of spices stirred in.

Without a sign, a house, a roadside tree, any fixed object, it was near impossible to reckon speed. The distant stars whose blurred images had traversed the cosmos from millions of light years away, were approached with infinitesimal slow progress. Ordinary senses could not be trusted. But one had to. That is all the perception man was given. Therefore, reason is required; reason and a body, brain, and cognizance. Humanity stepped out of dark ignorance when they began to make tools and take the measure of things. It was man's quest of extracting useful knowledge out of the infinite.

The ionic rockets of Starfarer were the most advanced mode of propulsion thus far invented. The spaceship corkscrewed through the galaxy at a speed too dizzying to imagine. To even think of a sharp turn was to already have passed the turning point. Steering was begun from nearly incomprehensible distances away from target. The destination they strove for— a livable planet in some galaxy somewhere off in the vast cosmos.

Space itself defies description. How does one grasp the concept of a galaxy? Think of a huge star speeding through space at tremendous velocity ringed by planets, moons, and zillions of meteors and asteroids— a dazzling flaring fireworks display in motion. Stars, sometimes multiple stars, some engulfed in nebular clouds and dust with comets zooming by them. How can a fragment contemplate this immensity?

Magical thinking doesn't get you there. Dreams are insufficient. Only exploration has led humanity forward. As pioneers of yore, the Starfarer astronauts were streaking through the vast immensity and risking all— life, liberty, and in pursuit of what? A new life; an answer to the age-old question, are we alone in the universe?

Over the Starfarer radio came a crackly sound. It was Kronkite calling. He radioed and persisted with his usual dogged questioning. In the past, Atom had acutely felt Kronkite's superior status— teacher to student, boss to worker, mentor to protégé, celebrity to a nobody, father-figure to son. Even at the distance of billions of miles, the habit remained. In the last few months, however, a new sense of command was growing in Atom.

Atom continued to seek advice, compare notes with ground control, and discuss technicalities with the engineering experts. He was open to suggestions and eager for opinions. Still, inside he was feeling new competence that he had never felt before.

Kronkite pressed Atom about Orwell and Darla with direct and searching questions. While Atom's mind was filled with navigational calculations for the next planetary intersection, he explained that, as far as he could determine, Orwell and Darla had gone through a marital problem, but now all was resolved. That was it. If Kronkite insisted on pursuing it further, he would have to ask Orwell directly. Atom did, however, mention to Kronkite that perhaps losing the digital streaming of sport broadcasts might have put Orwell in a bad mood. He had since begun to watch movies for diversion.

That was how communication with ground control ended. Atom was happy with his assertiveness in coping with Kronkite's relentless probing, but it left him with a weariness of heart.

He was struck with the word '*ground*'. A base, a foundation. Something solid and firm. He thought back to his old home planet, and somehow the word was losing its old meaning. Everything in space was flying, there was nothing firm in the firmament. Ground was a figment of the imagination, gravity a local condition.

Atom put down his charting instruments and looked around at the dark enclosing cold metal walls. Behind the veneer of paint and plastic was barely concealed the structure of the spaceship. The cold, artificial diode lights cast shadows everywhere. In the eternal night of space, he tried to summon a memory of daylight. How was it sitting on a porch, hiking in the woods, standing in a field? Such commonplaces, so remote from him now.

He decided to visit Evelyn. He walked down the hallways of the three Zones, till he reached the greenhouse.

The greenhouse was indeed green. It would be a misnomer, however, to think of it as typical of a normal land-based greenhouse. This one admitted no outside light. There was none. It was not a glassed-in enclosure. It was artificially lit. It was merely a large area in which to house and grow plants. Besides furnishing food and air for the astronauts, it provided an essential relief from their claustrophobic quarters and the infinite blackness of

72

space-night outside. It was the largest compartment in the spaceship, and it was alternately lit and darkened to simulate ordinary growing and resting cycles. It hardly resembled the out-of-doors of the home planet they'd left.

Although in the greenhouse every effort had been made to create the appearance of a nature trail, it hardly sufficed. The brilliance of the lights and the shimmer of its greenery coupled with its aromatic atmosphere, did serve somewhat as an anti-depressant to raise the astronaut's spirits. Tending the plants was a particularly soothing, relaxing and beneficial duty. It simulated a bit what earthbound gardeners enjoy. But it was not at all like communing with Nature. It was too factory-like.

Despite an effort to create the appearance of a nature trail, it didn't make it. The brilliant lights made it too artificial.

At Sara's urging, the designers did everything possible, within structural and weight restrictions, to dispel the rigid functionality of the greenhouse. They tried to create an illusion of a wilderness place. Plant supports were disguised as spiraling tendrils. Trickling fountains were faked. A sound track of bird songs, and whispering breeze was provided. But after a while the repetitive recording, became annoying to Evelyn and she silenced it. Only the light cycles continued.

It would have to serve as a semblance of outdoors while the astronauts were on their long voyage, confined as they were in Starfarer. If they never reached a habitable planet, it would have to serve as their outdoors for life.

Walking along among the plants, Atom found Evelyn and Darla together. Evelyn was planting some seedlings and Darla was helping.

"How are you little farmerettes doing?" asked Atom.

"Good enough," said Evelyn. "Or rather, I should say, *good*. Kronkite lectured me once, that good enough is not good enough. It's either good or it *isn't good*. In any case, I'm pleased with the little seedlings. They're off to a good start. Darla just naturally has a green thumb."

"More like dirty brown fingernails," quipped Darla. "I keep forgetting the gardening gloves."

"It makes you a part of the growing process, digging in with your fingers like that," said Atom.

"Yes," Evelyn scolded, "but don't walk off with any of my good soil. That's valuable stuff here. And it's not easy to hail down a passing meteor to replenish our supply."

Atom joined Evelyn and Darla in the gardening task. It helped him take his mind off the coming planetary interception.

CHAPTER XIV

Months had passed, and the U-5 planet intersect was imminent. The astronauts had ridden "the can" up to the pilothouse. If television transmission could be maintained, this would be another newsworthy event. The astronauts were buckled into their seats prepared for the flyby.

"Be ready. We're getting close," cautioned Atom focused as U-5 came into view.

At first, it wasn't immediately apparent to them because it blended into the starry background. Fast approaching it, what finally made it stand out, was its spinning motion in orbit. Then it became massive in their sight. Its two moons could be seen casting a shadow across its bulging equator.

"Planet U-4, which we bypassed, was 92,000 miles across and made a complete rotation in a little over eight hours," said Atom.

"It would be terrific getting paid by the day, there. The old paycheck would really mount up, wouldn't it?" said Orwell.

"Sure, but think of it," said Darla, "four hours of daylight and four hours of night. You'd hardly wake up before you'd be getting ready for bed again."

"I wonder how plants would adapt to that schedule. I might set aside a small section for an experiment to see how our leafy friends would adjust to it. Could they grow, survive, or even thrive on a four-hour light schedule? How would it affect the plants growth rate?"

Evelyn was already, in her mind, setting up an apparatus for such an experimental study.

"It might work for instant oats," joked Orwell.

All smiled. It was a tension-relieving comment.

Atom appreciated the quip because the danger they faced made him very tense. U-5 was now in sight. Starfarer was approaching U-5 rapidly; the planet he hoped to get a gravity propulsion assist from. What he was feeling was the difference between driving in the country compared to the stress felt during rush hour traffic. Except worse.

"Watch the radar, Orwell," said Atom. "S'far as I know, U-5 has only two large-sized moons, but it also has quite a retinue of smaller captured satellites. Beyond that, however, I can't be sure what else we might encounter. I don't want to use the phrase 'run into', you know what I mean?"

The planet they were fast approaching was mammoth. It was more than twice the size of all the planets in their planetary system.

"Planet U-5 orbits once in a decade, or roughly takes ten times more than ours did to make a single orbit," said Atom. "Naturally, its elliptical orbit is much larger than our own."

Now U-5 stood out brightly from its speckled star black background. It was like a huge ball being thrown at one, except this one was far too large to be caught.

"Kronkite calling Starfarer. Are you receiving me? Over."

Since Atom was at the controls of the spaceship, Darla took the radio call.

"This is Starfarer. Darla speaking. Over."

"Hell-oo, Darla," replied Kronkite. "Good to hear your voice. Have you spotted planet U-5 yet? If the television transmission works, we're hoping to get a good view of it. Over."

"We're closing in on it now. We're transmitting, can you see it? It's huge. Over."

"No," said Kronkite. "We're encountering picture interference from some source. Probably static emissions from U-5's strong magnetic field. Over."

"I hope you get a view of it. It looks spectacular. It resembles a big hot ball candy with swirls in it." described Darla. "It's not dead-looking, like the first planet we flew by. And it's definitely not as cool or friendly-looking as our own planet. It's growing in size, and its rotation is bearing down on us. Over."

"Must be a thrilling sight, Darla. We'll stand by. Keep us informed as things develop. The technicians are working on the picture reception problem. Over and out."

U-5's size now filled the height of Starfarer's window frame. Its enormous rotational speed could be observed as its moons and features appeared and raced across its surface. U-5's most prominent features were the bands of fiery swirling vortex of clouds and gas. It was a planet of cyclones and stormy turbulence. It was animated with bursts of volcanic-like flame, except for its polar regions. Overall, it was a total conflagration.

"Wow! Now I know how a ladybug would feel seeing a stampeding elephant coming at her." said Orwell. "And this one is inflamed, besides."

"Anything showing on radar?"

"All clear so far, Atom."

Now the surface of U-5 filled the entire view of Starfarer's window from side to side. The whole planet was ablaze, as if totally engulfed in a massive forest fire. Evelyn winced at the sight of it.

"What an unfriendly planet for plants," she thought. "Deserts could be made to bloom with watering and fertilization, but nothing could likely live on this scorching sizzling planet."

"I wouldn't look for any landing place down there," Orwell said. "No place for an airport."

"Get ready," Atom warned. "Here we go!"

Gripping the controls, Atom prepared to make the gravity assist maneuver. A miscalculation and Starfarer could be drawn into the furnace maelstrom. It was at that very instant that they witnessed a gaseous explosion erupt from U-5's surface. They could see a bubbling cloud gushing up.

"Radar warning!" shouted Orwell.

Atom looked quickly at the radar and then back at U-5. The explosion ahead was shooting a cloud into Starfarer's path. No time to veer and steer clear. "Hold on, everyone!" Atom called out. "We're in for a bumpy ride!"

They froze in their seats. They cringed as the cloud's debris— pounding like hail on a tin roof— raked the ship's hull. They were unavoidably exposed to the danger by the ship's trajectory. They feared U-5's gravity would pull them into its flaming atmosphere. They shuddered at the thought that this crematorium would be their final planetary home.

An instant after the bombardment had strafed their hull, Starfarer sped out of the blinding cloud.

Atom gunned the rocket which slingshot them forward with breathtaking acceleration. From energy borrowed from the gravitational hub of the massive planet, they rebounded away from the broiling crimson bulk, and shot out once more into the emptiness of space.

"Wow," exclaimed Orwell, catching his breath, "that was some hug and kiss!"

Atom filled his lungs and slowly exhaled with a long sigh. "No way we're lining-up for another go-around back there."

"Another ride like that and I'd have to change my pants," said Orwell.

"I was surprised I was able to keep down my lunch," said Darla. "I think I could handle those run-of-the-mill carnival rides, now."

Evelyn sagged in her seat restraints to calm herself.

"Ground control probably wonders what happened," said Atom "Can you reach them, Darla?"

"Starfarer to Kronkite. Are you receiving us? Over."

The speaker crackled. "We're receiving you. We picked up your comments during the gravity assist. Did you suffer any damage? Over."

"Any condition you want to report, Atom?" asked Darla.

"No apparent damage. All controls functioning. Our course bearing is slightly skewed. I'm making corrections now."

"We made it intact. Over," reported Darla.

"Did you get any video of U-5?" asked Kronkite. "Over."

"Tell him we'll check when we're back in the control room," said Atom. "If we got any, we'll transmit it to him later. There was no time for observation. If we got some good images, he'll see why. Should be a thrilling sight. That eruption from U-5 really pelted us."

"Glad you're all safe," said Kronkite. "We'll wait for the replay. Over and out."

Starfarer was once again shooting off into the nowhere of space. As it sped out of the fringe of the galaxy, U-5, the huge volcanic planet, was rapidly shrinking from sight. One by one, Darla and Evelyn left the pilothouse and rode the can down to check the video footage and relay it back to Kronkite. Atom and Orwell were left to assess the damage, if any, from U-5's cloud.

The video of U-5 was spectacular. Relayed back, it was immediately broadcast around the globe, creating quite a stir. It was sensational for the public to see close-up views of U-5. For centuries, dreamers had created Olympian views of the heavens. They had portrayed them as a paradise populated by superhuman winged beings far superior to themselves. Now, for the first time, they were getting a glimpse of it as it actually is.

To the intelligent public, the cosmos was being demystified. A new lamp of knowledge was lighting the dark corners of mystery. More people everywhere were beginning to value science over occult thinking. Magazines heralded Atom, Evelyn, Orwell, and Darla as *The PEOPLE OF THE YEAR!*

The effect was far different for the astronauts. They had had a short personal experience with two planets. The one dead and, to all appearance, devoid of life. Blazing U-5 appeared totally hostile to anything living. Matter was scarce in the galaxy, and apparently, life was even more rare.

The day-to-day life for the astronauts was how to survive in a spaceship. As each day passed, they were growing less aware of public opinion. The glamour conferred by fame eluded them. There was nobody to fawn over them in space, no autograph hunters or pursuing press. Their celebrity was absorbed in survival in the deep silence of the cosmos.

CHAPTER XV

The debris from U-5's cloud eruption had raked the exterior of Starfarer. The question in Atom's mind was whether it had done any damage to their heat resistant shield. The exterior cameras didn't provide sufficient clarity to make that determination. For that reason, Atom decided one of them would have to don a space suit and go outside and make an inspection.

"I agree, I'll go," said Orwell. "Come to think of it, I haven't been outside in a long time."

They had just transmitted video views of planet U-5 to Kronkite. It was important that they were aware that Orwell was going outside the spaceship. This was not an everyday procedure.

They got Orwell's space suit out of the locker for the first time since launch. Donning the suit in the weightlessness of the pilothouse took some doing and required assistance. It was a rather comic scene.

"Damn, this suit has a mind of its own!" said Orwell as he and the suit did pirouettes. "This crazy task is one Kronkite didn't plan well, and we sure don't have time to rehearse it."

"I agree," said Atom, amused by Orwell's antics. "Just goes to show, it's easier to peel an orange than put the peel back on."

Finally, by improvising— attaching some seat belts to the suit— they were able to get his feet in the trousers and his arms in the sleeves. It was a clumsy operation suiting-up, but with help it was accomplished.

Next, they attached the helmet with the breathing apparatus. Orwell then entered the small airlock compartment at the pilothouse portal which he had entered so very long ago. Soon, he was floating like a large bird of prey on the outside of Starfarer. For safety, he was attached to a tether so he could not put too much distance between himself and the fuselage. Darla and Evelyn joined Atom in the pilothouse and were watching Orwell check the hull for damage to the ship that might have resulted from the U-5 incident.

"How does it look?" asked Atom over the intercom.

"Pitted, but not seriously compromised," replied Orwell. "I'll apply a little of this acne cream goo, and it should be pretty enough for a senior prom dance."

They all enjoyed Orwell's joking comment.

The time passed very quickly. Atom pointed to his watch held to the window and said, "Better finish up now. Your time's almost up."

Orwell nodded. "I finished the repair," he said. He made his way back into the decompression chamber. As this was the first attempt at outside maintenance repair, it had worked incredibly well.

Atom worked the valves that equalized atmospheric pressure to the hatch compartment. Darla was smiling at Orwell through the door window.

"We'll have a nice meal soon," she said through the glass.

Orwell gestured her a thumbs-up.

The pressure came to parity, and Atom turned the unlocking handles. Nothing happened! He tried again. A wrinkle of annoyance crossed his brows. Putting more effort into it— being weightless— only caused his body to react in the opposite direction.

"What's the matter?" asked Evelyn, realizing that something was wrong.

"The catch…is not releasing," said Atom.

Together, they both attempted to turn the handles. The handles wouldn't budge.

Orwell, inside the chamber, could see that there was some difficulty.

"What's wrong?" he asked through the intercom.

"Can't get this to release," said Atom. "Grab your handles. We'll try to turn them together."

Both men braced and put muscle into it, but the latches wouldn't give.

Orwell was starting to get panicky.

"Evelyn, ride the can down and bring me back some tools."

"What tools do you want?"

"Mainly wrenches, a crowbar, and a hammer. You know where they are, don't you?"

"Yes. I'll be right back," she said. She took the tube elevator down.

Darla looked through the window at Orwell struggling with the handles, and tried her luck. There was no turning them.

Orwell was becoming agitated. "I'm beginning to feel like a turkey in an oven," he said rather humorlessly. The small space in the chamber was beginning to get to him.

"Be patient. Save your energy. Evelyn's gone to get some tools," said Atom.

"You're beginning to sound more like Kronkite every day," said Orwell in a rather uncomplimentary tone of voice.

Mentally, Atom was scratching his head at the situation. The gauge clearly indicated that pressure was equalized, but some intuition caused him to question it. He tapped the gauge lightly with his fingertips. The indicator dropped. The pressure had not equalized. The dial had stuck.

Atom immediately knew what that meant. Starfarer's atmosphere had not entered the chamber.

Orwell was still dependent on his suit for breathing. His air supply was nearly exhausted.

Evelyn arrived with the tools. There was no way force would open the door. The pressure differential was too great.

"Orwell, stay calm. Conserve as much air as you can. Do you hear me?" ordered Atom. "The gauge was stuck. The air exchange didn't take place."

Orwell looked livid. He was really becoming upset…"It didn't work? What d'ya mean it didn't work?"

"The air input is open, but the air is not flowing through. It's pumping as hard as it can. Something is obstructing it."

"Damn it! Beat it with a hammer or something!" yelled Orwell.

Atom touched the pump and quickly snatched his fingers away. It was getting too hot to touch. It would soon burn out or blow a circuit. He pressed his face to the glass to see into the chamber.

Atom tapped on the glass. "Orwell!" he said pointing to the side of the chamber. "Check that opening. Is something blocking it?"

"What d'ya mean?"

"I mean, see if it's clogged up."

Orwell worked his gloved fingers at the cavity opening.

All of a sudden, there was a violent whoosh of air, and a puff of dust filled the chamber. A steady flow of air began to hiss inside it. The gauge began to react normally.

The tension wreaked havoc with Atom's nerves. He was relieved, nonetheless, that he had discovered the problem. Now, if they were only in time to save Orwell. Soon, the pressure equalized. He forced open the door and hauled Orwell inside and quickly opened his face mask. Minutes more and he would have suffocated.

The three of them buckled Orwell into one of the seats. He puffed in huge gulps of air. His eyelids drooped and opened slowly as he revived. He had been so close to asphyxiation that the terror of it had left him completely drained of energy.

"I'll take…that meal…now," he said, much subdued.

The entire incident was probably related to the erupting cloud incident. U-5's dust had somehow permeated the chamber and been sucked into the air nozzle, plugging it up. Together they had faced death during the launch. Besides the U-5 incident, this was the closest one of them had faced it since.

They could never forget that they carried their living atmosphere with them and were totally dependent on it. They were attached to their flying island by a thread— the next breath of air.

Orwell's disposition had been altered drastically again. He became withdrawn, taciturn, no longer talkative. He spent a lot of his time watching movies, one after another. Everyone was careful not to tread on his mood. Younger than Atom, he seemed to have aged beyond his years. He became inattentive to Darla and she would confide her hurt to Atom. He would feel powerless to affect a solution and the situation continued unresolved.

Basically, it came down to this: Orwell recognized he had a problem, but in the same breath, denied having any. Nor would he accept or welcome advice or seek a remedy. He seemed to luxuriate in the attention it brought him, rather than truly be motivated toward any solution. So, he swung from lighthearted to moody constantly. Both, in effect, got him sympathetic attention. Atom wondered if that was what Orwell wanted.

Despite Orwell's mercurial mood swings, the Starfarer routines had to go on, regardless. Atom was making final navigational calculations for their last destination. It was the outer-most orbiting planet of their galactic system. Since it was small and most distant of all, little was known about it. Did it have an atmosphere? Was it habitable? Nobody knew. At its distance, the expectation was that it would be quite cold. But that hadn't been confirmed. Observing it up close, it was hoped would answer some questions about it.

One day, Darla came up to Atom as he was bent over his charts in the control room.

"I have some news," she said.

"*Good* news, I hope," said Atom.

"I hope it is," Darla said. "I've picked up some radio signals on the ROSS scanner. It's in no language that we know, but it's definitely not static."

"That *is* good news. Let me know when you hear it again. I'll listen with you."

CHAPTER XVI

Each day, Starfarer made more progress toward the outermost planet. It was the last known planet of their solar system. It would be the last hope for them that it or any nearby satellite moon might furnish the astronauts a home to live on.

Three or more times a day Atom checked his navigational reckonings. One day he was greeted with a gigantic meteor streaking across the surveillance screen. It was shaped like a huge potato. He called the others and they hurried to see it. It was an awesome sight because of its size. It was probably a mixture of ice, iron, and stone. One could almost imagine riding it across space.

"That may be our first interstellar visitor," said Atom. "It could have come from another galaxy. Meteors are renegades. They seem to make their own path and not belong anywhere in particular. They don't seem to be a part of anything. They seem to be loners, flying freely and unhindered until they meet their demise— either burning up or crashing."

"Fortunately," said Evelyn, "the cosmos is as large as it is, with so many meteors loose in space."

"Too bad we can't harness one. It would sure add to our horse power," said Orwell. Several weeks had passed since the air-lock incident. Orwell was once more his old congenial self.

"A planet without an atmosphere would be devastated, if struck by that meteor," said Atom. However, the odds of that happening are unlikely. Still, it could happen. That's why we must remain vigilant. A lone meteor could destroy us, and it wouldn't have to be a large one to do it."

"Yeah," said Orwell. "One could hit back home and wipe out everybody. Then we'd be the lucky ones. We'd be the only survivors. The joke would be on them. Wouldn't that be something? Us, the only survivors?"

"I wouldn't wish that," said Atom. "No doubt, meteors are dangerous, though. We must be alert."

"Wonder where that meteor was headed?" said Orwell. "Maybe to visit Kronkite. Wouldn't that be something? We could have put a message on it for him. 'With love to Sara'."

No one was amused by Orwell's remark. It was an edgy comment;

seemed somewhat sinister. Orwell shrugged off the silence and continued talking. "It did look like a potato. You know, I could have made a fortune selling tickets to see that big flying rock."

"And I would help you spend it," said Darla entering the conversation.

"I'm sure you would. That's the only advantage being here. There isn't a shopping mall around every corner," Orwell rambled on. "Just think, with all we're saving put out at compound interest, I'd be a millionaire. That is if I had a paying job. When we get to where we're going and it's uninhabited, I want first chance at owning the bank. Yes sir, I want to be the banker."

Lacking seasonal changes, the meteor was a momentary diversion in their drab daily lives. Orwell left to watch canned movies on his time off. Sometimes the views of his old life cheered him, other times it made him gloomy. Darla was spending much of her time at the ROSS scanner. She had found a frequency that had some promising radio signals. She was trying to analyze them for message content. Daily, without fail, Evelyn was in the greenhouse. The plants provided her family. She doted on them like a hen might her chicks. If not a plant physiologist, she would have been an avid backyard gardener. Every time they enjoyed her bee's honey, Evelyn felt especially proud.

Atom entered the control room. He found Darla busy as usual at the radio console.

"Oh, Atom. I'm glad you're here. Listen to this."

Atom cocked his head to one side as Darla adjusted the radio dials. A pattern of sound came from the speaker. It was not a voice, but it had variations which suggested a coded message of some kind.

"Have you been able to decipher anything out of it yet?" asked Atom.

"Nothing yet," said Darla, listening intently. "I'm running an analysis through the computer to isolate frequent patterns and contextual divisions."

"Good," said Atom. "Sounds promising. How are things with you and Orwell lately?"

"Quite good, thanks. I guess it's not unusual for people to have their ups and downs."

"I know what you mean," said Atom. "I get in a rut myself some days. Say, do you think those radio signals are coming from the planet ahead? That would be great."

"That's a strong possibility, and that's why I'm particularly excited."

"I really appreciate your spending all this additional time radio-monitoring. It's not required of you, you know."

"That's all right, Atom. I don't mind doing it, and I enjoy spending time with you. The movies start to bore me after a while, and I'm not much for exercise or gardening. Who needs all that back pain and dirt?"

"I should be getting more exercise myself," said Atom. "I'm getting out of shape. I get my backaches bending over this chart table."

"Kronkite calling Starfarer. Are you receiving me? Over."

"There's Kronkite on the horn. Switch over and we'll see what he has to say. Also, see if you can increase the volume. His voice is sounding very weak."

"I'll try to amplify it. I've noticed lately that we've begun to reach the outer-limits of the signal."

"Atom and Darla here. Receiving you. Can you speak louder? Over."

"I'll try. At 12:45 our time, tomorrow, I want to transmit a compressed voice microchip to you. Our transmitting satellite will be directly in line with you then. Can you be set to receive it? Over."

"Darla?"

"Yes, we can be ready," she answered.

Lately, extended communication had grown very difficult. They experienced frequent interference and fading. There was only a small window when ground control could establish a direct connection to Starfarer.

"Darla says she can be ready. What's the message about? Over."

"Please repeat. I couldn't make out your answer. Over."

"Yes, Darla will be ready." Atom articulated each syllable very distinctly. "What is it you are sending us?"

"The chip will contain some views I've compiled over my lifetime. I hope they will proo-oo...." At this moment, humming and crackling broke into the message.

"We've lost your voice, Kronkite!" called Atom. "Repeat, please. Over."

"I'm afraid we've lost him for today," said Darla, trying to squelch the static without success.

"I'll set the recorder to pick up the chip message at 12:45 their time. If it's clean, we should be able to do it. I wonder what he'll be sending to us."

"I do, too," said Atom. "I'm sure with him it will be detailed and thoroughly thought through. You know Kronkite."

"Kronkite didn't ask about U-9, our next planet rendezvous. Do you think they're losing interest in the project?" asked Darla.

"Hard to say. The public does have a short attention span. U-9 is more remote and a smaller planet, and likely won't be as spectacular or grandiose as U-5 was. If it doesn't have a fast food restaurant on it, who knows, it may not get much attention at all."

"You're sounding like Orwell. But really, why would a small planet get less attention than a larger one? That doesn't give little gals much hope," said Darla with a wink.

84

"Present little gals exempted, of course," smiled Atom. "That is a matter of aesthetics. A gem obviously has more value than a boulder."

"I'm glad to hear that," smiled Darla.

"It happens more with intangibles, such as ideas. Little facts don't carry much weight when people crave giant-sized claims. It's always easier to grab attention with exaggeration than intelligence.

Glitter trumps common sense."

"That's pretty pessimistic, Atom."

"I don't mean to make it sound that way. It's natural for our species to seek the easy way. And, paradoxically, it's probably the reason for all our technology. What other creature works so hard to make things easy? Can you think of one? We work hard to invent machines to do our work for us. What other creature works so hard to make things easy, instead of basically just living?"

"That is strange," reflected Darla. "Does that explain Kronkite's motivation?"

"That's a good question. You've got me there. Maybe we'll find out tomorrow."

CHAPTER XVII

At 12:45 ground time precisely, a voice microchip was transmitted to and recorded by Darla on Starfarer. It was increasingly difficult to communicate with Kronkite on the astronaut's former planet. The distance for such radio calls was becoming a barrier. There was only one small window that conversations relayed via satellite could be carried on. Thus, a communication gap was developing.

On the positive side, the astronauts were to be the first ever to view the most distant planet at the outer edge of their planetary system. It hadn't been discovered by observers with telescope for centuries. Eyewitness reports from the astronauts would be invaluable.

Top of Atom's list was, would the planet be habitable? Would it have water, and atmosphere, and life? Did it have potential for colonization? Within days they would have their answer.

What was in the mind of each astronaut was not known. They hadn't spent any time sharing their hopes, expectations, or fears. Much of the vagueness stemmed back to the rather ambiguous purpose of the Starfarer project. There was no doubt the project was a success in collecting data that had been beamed back. Scientists would be evaluating the new knowledge for years to come.

What about the astronauts? How were they to benefit? Or were they merely expendable like test pilots?

Atom wasn't sure, but he thought perhaps Kronkite's microchip might supply some answers.

Hope must be a vital component in the existence of a thoughtful person. Usually a strong instinct to survive persists, no matter how dreary the present life, how abysmal the circumstances.

Hope then functions as a kind of lottery. It's that future out there that's going to arrive and going to be good even though the present may now seem unsatisfactory. It's that counterbalance to things as they are, to things as one wants them to be.

Is hope then a delusion? Or is it merely an unfulfilled reality?

Right now, Atom and the others were living on hope. Adventure and the promise of something better kept them going. It didn't hurt to be first at something. That sought-after-thing called accomplishment. At this moment of their lives, hope was embodied in the one last planet.

Atom entered the control room to do his routine navigational check of the autopilot. Darla was sitting at the radio console.

"How is the decoding going? Make any headway on the signals?"

"It turned out to be just a false alarm," said Darla without her usual sparkle. "After spending several days of trying to find a pattern, a syntax, a grammar— anything that would give the sound meaning, I've come to the conclusion it's not any kind of broadcast after all."

"What is it, then?"

"I believe now that it was nothing more than X-ray emissions from an exploding star behind the planet, way out in the cosmos."

Atom put his hand on Darla's shoulder. "So, they're not sending us a welcoming greeting. We just have to arrive unannounced, that's all. Don't let it get you down."

Darla appreciated the reassurance, smiled, and touched her cheek to Atom's hand as it rested on her shoulder.

"Come, take a look at planet U-9. It's now in sight. Just around the bend, so to speak."

They stood together looking at the surveillance screen— a great black curtain with polka dots of sparkling lights.

"What would it be like to examine all those stars in space forever?" asked Darla.

"Now, there's a thought," said Atom. "What *would* it be like?" He thought about it a second.

"It'd be something like being on a beach, and examining all sand one grain at a time."

"That's not a very romantic view of it," said Darla. "That would be all work and no play. Just another job."

"More than that. Hypothetically, it'd be a life-long career. Pragmatically, I'm only interested in one thing— finding a livable planet. Isn't that your hope, too?"

"Yes, I suppose it is," she said, without much conviction. "Mostly, I think I live one day at a time— live for now."

For Darla, hope was attention and atmosphere. She required little. Much of what she craved was satisfied simply— in a kind word, a smile, a touch, a feeling that she was wanted and needed.

Of the four astronauts, she was the one with a decorator's touch. Because of weight limitations on Starfarer, they had been severely restricted as to the quantity of personal belongings they could bring aboard. Of the four, Darla had the largest portion devoted to objects, stuffed animals, wall hangings, and the like. Once airborne with centrifugal gravity, she took particular pains to decorate the compartment she and Orwell shared. It gave her spirits a lift.

Orwell was amused by, but didn't share her interest in, such objects. A large portion of his discretionary luggage was devoted to some sports memorabilia and additional movies for recreation. Orwell was an avid fan of action and adventure films.

Despite the fact that a large proportion of weight was already devoted to the greenhouse, an additional portion of Evelyn's allowance consisted of bulbs and roots. Some were unusual food plants. The flowers were sufficient to satisfy her need for color, her decorative sense. Not much space could be devoted to growing them, but the little that was available served the need for beauty in Evelyn's life. She was one of those fortunate people whose work and avocation were one.

In Atom's allowance was a music system and collection of recorded music. Music had been one of his joys back home. Since launch, he had not listened to music once. Had he lost interest in it or was he too heavily absorbed in his responsibilities? Whatever the reason, his favorite music was ignored.

Now in space, there were choices each astronaut could make and conditions each had to accept.

Atom showed Darla where they should intersect with their last planet in two days. She was very attentive as he pointed out a tentative destination on the chart.

"That's very interesting," she said. "Not exactly like going by GPS. You'll have to teach me more about it. Remember Kronkite said we were supposed to learn each other's skills."

"That's right. I'd be glad to teach you. Next time I'm making the calculations, and you're free, I'll show you how it's done," said Atom, pleased that she had taken an interest in navigation.

"Okay. Let me know when."

"I will. But since this is your time-off, why don't you take a rest from the ROSS scanner today," suggested Atom. "You've put in a lot of extra time as it is."

"I don't mind doing it," said Darla.

"I know you don't, but no sense in overdoing it."

In the meantime, Orwell was engrossed in an action thriller. He had his shoes off, his feet propped up, stretched out on the couch. It was not a couch in the usual sense. All the furnishings were fastened to the ship, not pieces of furniture one would find in a home. Darla entered, at first unseen.

"Oh," said Orwell, "I didn't see you come in, honey."

"I know. I didn't want to interrupt your show."

"That's okay, I can pause it. Come over and watch it with me. I'll fill you in on the plot."

"That's all right. I'm going back to the room and slip into something more comfortable." Orwell sensed a certain reticence in her, or at least, he thought he did. "You're spending an awful lot of time up in the control room, aren't you?"

"Yes, I've been analyzing some radio signals from space."

"And what did you find out?"

"Nothing. They may only be X-ray emissions from an exploding star."

"All that, for nothing?" said Orwell.

Darla shrugged off his question. "I'm going back to the room. Coming along soon?"

"Soon as this is over." Orwell pushed *PLAY,* starting the movie again. Darla left, closing the rec. room door very softly.

In the greenhouse, Evelyn was pruning one of her flowering plants when Atom joined her. She stood back, head to one side, and studied her work. "How's it look?" she asked.

"Beautiful, sweetheart. How could it be anything else with all the attention you lavish on it." Atom embraced her and gave her a kiss.

"Watch out for my shears," she cautioned.

"I will," he said with a smile. "You're a dangerous woman, you know that?"

"Not really. Not until I'm riled," she laughed. "Has Darla had any luck yet?"

"With what?"

"You told me she was decoding some promising radio signal from space."

"Oh, those. No, she's pretty disappointed about it, too. After further consideration, she believes it to be only X-ray emissions."

"Sorry to hear that."

"Yeah, it was a big letdown for her," said Atom. "You know, it's almost lunch time."

"You can go ahead if you want to."

"No, I'll wait. Don't forget," he continued, "in a couple of days, you'll have to take time away from the greenhouse. We've got another space rendezvous coming up."

"Thanks for reminding me," Evelyn said. "I hope that next planet will be a green one."

"Me too, sweetie," said Atom. "Me, too."

"Sure, you want to wait till I finish here?" she asked. "You could go relax a bit."

"No that's all right. Can I give you a hand planting that?"

"No, really I'm almost finished," said Evelyn putting her trowel down.

"Don't hurry, I can wait." said Atom admiring a plant. "I'll just visit your plants and we can go to lunch together."

89

CHAPTER XVIII

Atom had one more day to wait until his third planet rendezvous. Approaching a planet intersect always caused him to lose sleep and feel nervous. His adrenalin kept him tense but at least experience had given him more confidence.

This planet was the furthest out and the least known. It was a small planet with a very large elliptical orbit. For such a small planet, the big question was— would it be friendly to life? It would be their last chance in their own galaxy.

Atom double checked for navigation errors— the Kronkite way.

That afternoon he tried to divert his mind by visiting Evelyn in the greenhouse and offering to help her tend the plants.

"Careful," she said. "You're not watching where you step. You're stepping on that vine."

"Sorry, sweetheart. My mind is just too preoccupied, I guess."

"You didn't sleep well last night. You kept tossing and turning. Why don't you take a nap, or go watch one of Orwell's movies or something?"

"You know what I think I'll do? I'll go listen to some music. I haven't listened to my sound system at all. Not even once."

"That's a good idea," Evelyn said. "I'll see you later for dinner and maybe listen to some music with you."

"Atom went back to their room and played one of his favorite songs. He sat down and tried to make himself comfortable and listen. The music played, but his mind wandered. Soon he realized it was hopeless. He wasn't hearing the music at all or enjoying it. Then a thought came to him. Kronkite's microchip. Being curious about what it contained certainly engaged his mind. It was like a sealed package that keeps beckoning to be opened.

The microchip had been put into Starfarer's library. Atom walked through the control room to the library. Evelyn was still in the greenhouse. Orwell and Darla, because of the split-shift, would be asleep. So no one was about.

Before he could listen to it, he took one more check of their course. It was sort of like when he was at home he'd check to see if lights were left on and the backdoor locked. Starfarer was still on course. He returned to the library and plugged Kronkite's message into the player.

What had Kronkite said? Was it something or other about a code? Kronkite's invention had already had a huge impact on society with his Verity Scanner exposing sham, deception, and lies. What could he add to that? Whatever it was, Kronkite had taken pains to transmit it on the most advanced delivery system— a compressed-voice microchip.

Atom, pushed the *PLAY* button, adjusted the volume, and sat close to the speaker to listen.

"Dear Starfarer astronauts," Atom recognized Kronkite's voice at once, *"I want you to know how proud we are of you,... all of you. These are my thoughts from my long life which I wish to share with you. Thoughts I want you to share with others as well. Challenge the ideas, if you like. Freedom thrives and improves by being challenged. That is the path to wisdom.*

In mankind's past, not believing in yourself was wisdom. Heroism was killing and silencing opponents. Obedience was owed to fake prophets. Those ancient fakers were wrong. The Verity Scanner has revealed them to be false.

True love cannot be demanded or owed. The only true love is love that is freely given without obligation or compulsion.

Wisdom is learning to believe in yourself. You were not born bad. Who can you trust if you can't trust yourself? A real honest person knows his own honesty and displays it.

Finally, heroism is a noble act, a kind act, an act of courage and worth. Murder is none of these. Therefore, killing is not heroic.

Take the time to examine these statements and consider whether they are true for you."

Atom sat back in his seat. He had expected encouragement, perhaps a pep talk, maybe technical advice from Kronkite— not what he was hearing.

He wasn't sure what he was to do specifically with the information. Kronkite was not a person to mince words. Everything he did was deliberate and purposeful. He had accomplished much in his lifetime. What he said did square with how he conducted his life.

Whatever Kronkite's intent, at least it was a diversion from Atom's anxiety about Starfarer's rendezvous with planet U-9 tomorrow.

Atom could hardly wait to share Kronkite's words with the others, especially Evelyn. He considered waiting till he could share the microchip with the others but his curiosity got the better of him. He pushed the *PLAY* button to hear the second part. Kronkite's voice came on as before.

"The following are virtues and vices that I have compiled over a lifetime and I have one request to make of all my listeners whoever they may be. Accept nothing on faith. Challenge everything stated here. A cutting edge sharpens itself by facing abrasion. If you are ready,

continue." Kronkite's voice proclaimed.

Atom felt himself almost talking to Kronkite, his presence was so strongly felt. It was almost as if he was actually in the library with him. Atom nearly answered that he was ready.

"*The first list I will give you,*" said Kronkite's voice, "*is that of the seven vices. They are:*"

1. *Unhealthy addictions*
2. *Thievery*
3. *Pride in ignorance*
4. *Mental and physical sloth*
5. *Lying*
6. *Teaching superstition*
7. *Preaching hatred*

"*You may take time to consider this list before continuing,*" says Kronkite.

Atom reflected on the list and considered jotting them down for further study. It was Kronkite through and true. He wondered how he was supposed to use the list. Could you prevent such vices? Indeed, were they preventable?

Generally, Atom didn't like to think in negative terms. Having heard the list, he began to wonder what the seven virtues would be. He was tempted to stop the player and make up a list of his own. However, his curiosity overwhelmed him, so he started the player again.

"*You have heard the seven vices,*" continued Kronkite's voice, "*these are the seven virtues:*"

1. *Healthy habits.*
2. *Empathy & tolerance*
3. *Perception & discernment*
4. *Inquiring mind*
5. *Acquired knowledge*
6. *Exuded optimism*
7. *Civility & friendship*

The list surprised Atom. He had not known that Kronkite, the man of action, was so philosophical. If those qualities were possible, wouldn't they make a wonderful society— an enlightened society? Was that too pie-in-the sky? Would such a society be possible? It was something to think about.

Atom switched off the player. Kronkite's message had given him much to think about. He was looking forward to sharing it with Evelyn, Darla, and Orwell, and getting their reactions to it. It had worked wonderfully to divert his mind and relieve the tension he felt at the coming planet rendezvous. Now he could go enjoy his dinner with Evelyn, and later maybe get some sleep.

CHAPTER XIX

When Atom revealed to Evelyn the contents of Kronkite's recorded voice message, she was likewise both impressed and confused. It was not like Kronkite. He was generally a man of projects, actions, and doing, not a man of reflection. He had led a productive life. It was not in his nature to have a philosophical turn of mind. His life had been spent in exploring material things, not words and thought. It was not a memoir which one might expect from a man his age. Nor, precisely, advice on how to get on, either. What did he have in mind?

Evelyn and Atom spent the evening discussing Kronkite's microchip message. They were particularly interested in what Kronkite called virtues. Why was *perception* grouped with *discernment*? How did one *exude optimism*? The list contained a wealth of thought for study. What significance did it have for the space pioneers? That, they couldn't figure out. Finally, they noticed the lateness of the hour. They would need their rest. They went to bed and quickly off to sleep. They wanted to be fresh for their next planet encounter.

*   *   *

"Evening, Ames," said Kronkite, as he sat down beside him at the radio console. "Any word yet from Starfarer?"

"None yet," replied Ames, eyeing the control panel. "Our rotation is just approaching window."

Window meant the most direct line from satellite transmitter to Starfarer.

Ames nodded his head thoughtfully. "I've been thinking about your idea for interplanetary relay satellites. I think it's good and possible. With each satellite tracking the orbit of the other, we could create a galactic network similar to cellphone towers. It would have great navigational possibilities, and communication ones, too. They would be space buoys for auto-piloting spacecraft.

"Good." Put it on the project list," said Kronkite. "Are we set for the video of the planet?"

"All set. Last time, planet U-5's magnetic field caused all the interference. Here, chances look good for a direct feed. All the television networks are standing by for a simulcast if— and that's a big *if*— we get a clear live signal. The news network is giving us almost continual coverage." Ames reached over and adjusted a dial.

"I'm amazed. To think we used to be just a blip on a newscast years ago. Nobody wanted even to cover us."

"It is amazing, isn't it? What grocery store tabloids used to sell as pseudo-science stuff, now science sells. People are demanding the truth, warts and all."

"You deserve the credit for that, Kronkite. The Verity Scanner gave fake news the kick in the butt it deserved. Then when the public insisted astrologers appear on television so they could be tested on home-model Verity Scanners, it drove the *horoscopes* off the market. Anyone with a kindergarten education learned that the prophets for profit were a sham-scam. The so-called 'stargazers' didn't know their planets from their asteroids."

Kronkite laughed. "It just goes to show, counterfeits are always bad currency. I think I'll try calling Atom. We might just pick him up if there isn't too much thermal deflection."

"Kronkite calling. Are you receiving me? Over."

They strained to listen. The only sound was a speaker softly hissing.

"Nothing," said Ames. "It's too soon. We'll try again in a few minutes."

Ames pivoted, stretched, and leaned back in his chair with hands cupped behind his head. "You know, it's almost unreal to think that they're out where they are far out in space. It took a lot of courage for them to sign on for this project."

"I wish I was with them, Ames. Risk is always a factor whether doing something, or doing nothing. I've always preferred doing something. It galls me that I was too old for Starfarer. I couldn't meet the criterion to be an astronaut, age-wise or physically. That's pretty sad, isn't it? I had a part in setting up the standards, and I couldn't pass them. If I could only do something about extending life."

"There's another project for your list, Kronkite," chuckled Ames.

The speaker crackled. Ames sat forward. Kronkite could hear a voice very indistinctly.

"Starfarer calling ground control. Can you hear us? Over."

"Hello, groundhogs, this is Orwell. Get ready. I'm patching the surveillance camera for simulcast. Are you getting a signal? Over."

A faint ghost of an image cast a shadow on the ground monitor's screen. Technicians with headsets were busily making adjustments all the while.

"That image is terrible," said Kronkite. "That's really going to disappoint viewers."

"Starfarer," radioed Ames, "what's your view? Over."

"We're approaching fast. Our picture is burning in clear as a diamond. Aren't you receiving anything yet?"

"Our picture is still unfocused and fuzzy, but with every rotation we're gaining better alignment. If your view is clear up there, can you give us any verbal observations? Have you spotted any moons?" asked Ames. "In the past, our astronomers aided by our largest telescopes have sighted only one. Over."

"Get out your pocket calculators, ladies and gentlemen, said Orwell. "Here are some numbers to add to your sky charts. I spot three moons, and there may be more on the blind side. With so many moons, this planet could be one heck of a romantic place. Over."

The ground crew had a hardy guffaw at Orwell's remark.

The reception quality of the television picture was still poor. Ames' assistant came up and asked:

"The networks are calling about the simulcast. What shall I tell them?"

"Tell them they can take some shots of the ground crew working, and fill with some interviews and commentary. That's the best we can do at the moment."

At the same time, ground control was agonizing over the poor picture quality. Ames was undergoing his own anxieties. Flying Starfarer into the vicinity of a planet was like skiing down a steep wooded slope in the dark, unable to stop, and not know what obstructions lay ahead.

Atom's concentration was so intense that he had left all the communicating to Orwell and Darla. He didn't want a repeat of their near disaster from the erupting cloud at the previous planet. Atom looked back at Evelyn. "Backup Orwell on checking the radar screen, will you?"

"What's the matter, don't you trust *me* to do it?" said Orwell rather peevishly. "Or maybe you blame me for that ash shower last time."

Atom was surprised by the curtness of Orwell's reply. It popped out of the blue, seemingly without reason.

"I wasn't thinking that at all. At this velocity, I can use all the eyes I can get. You already discovered more moons than we knew about before. There may be more. We're going to make a complete orbit of this planet. So, who can say what we'll meet up with?"

The exchange annoyed Atom who was already becoming tense as he tightly gripped the controls. There was no time to iron it out, however. The spaceship was beginning to conform to the surface of the slow spinning planet. They were not at all prepared for what they were about to see.

Their home planet that they had left, was one of beautiful oceans, land, and sky. They had passed two other planets. One that was small, stony, and desolate. Another that was huge, stormy, and a blazing inferno.

Beneath them was a bluish-white planet that resembled a snowball tossed by a giant. It was a completely frozen planet, ice-capped from pole to pole.

Orwell looked at it in dismay. No comic remark entered his mind or escaped his lips.

At that instant, a call came from ground control: "Kronkite calling Starfarer. The television picture is transmitting sharp and clear, you'll be pleased to know. You're getting worldwide coverage."

To the public, Starfarer's spectacular television views of the icy planet were a huge success. For a brief period, the picture quality was exceptionally good. Circling with one complete orbit, the viewer got to see its ice-infested equator. The planet was an ice palace. A glacier, an iceberg afloat in space. It was highly unlikely that complex forms of animals or plants could survive in its frigid temperature. It was entirely cold, barren, and uninhabitable.

"Well," said Orwell, rather gloomily, "that's the last house on the block."

The others knew what he meant. It was their last hope for a habitable planet in their own solar system. They would be moving on. They would be heading out into a void so vast, so empty, so devoid of matter, that crossing the largest ocean at home was a puny infinitesimal step by comparison.

They would be seeking a home on a new planet somewhere out among the big vacuum of space and star clusters.

When considering which destination to choose, from the myriad of choices, Atom at first had considered a binary star system, but crossed that off his list. He couldn't figure out what the effect of two suns would be. How would one cope with two rising and setting suns? If there were habitable planets, would the temperatures be extreme? How would anyone adapt to such a bizarre light interval that two suns might create? Maybe there would be no night at all. He would like to see such a system, of course, but travel did not permit that luxury.

Instead, Atom had set a course for a single star system that more nearly resembled the one they were leaving behind. It looked like their best hope. It was their *only* hope. Finding a habitable planet in the cosmos was a big gamble. The planet would have to have air they could breathe, water they could drink, food they could eat, and a favorable climate. It was an often-recurring question whether there were other celestial bodies that could support life. The destination Atom had plotted was millions of light-years away. At the moment, it was only a glittering speck.

They had the greatest rocket propulsion that technology and Kronkite could provide. Starfarer was a compact, self-contained living quarters. Properly maintained and navigated, it could survive the rigors of traveling distances in space. Still, as far as anyone knew, such a trek had never been made.

The most fragile elements aboard were the astronauts. It would take years to make the crossing to a new star system. The little icy planet offered them little borrowed energy for a gravity boost. They were left to their own resources. They would be without any outside help.

The longest trek of their journey lay ahead of them.

CHAPTER XX

After the planet of ice proved unfit for habitation came the realization they must look elsewhere for a home. They had found no planet in their solar system fit for them to occupy. As daunting as it was, they had to seek a new galaxy, a new planet. Hopefully, one which would have an atmosphere. This, it was understood, would be a journey never before attempted in the annals of humanity. It was a very sobering thought. Many immigrants have split families, leaving kin behind. But reunions were always possible. This migration was **final**.

En route, some radio contact with their home planet was still possible. They conferred with Kronkite regularly when conditions permitted. However, each day the radio signals were growing weaker, each day the contact grew shorter and more precious. Their few friends and family had said their last goodbyes already. It was a sorrowful parting. Newsmen vied with each other hoping to get interviews with the celebrated Starfarer crew. To the reporter's dismay, no time was available. The space traveler's celebrity remained news, but was fading. The Starfarer astronauts were vanishing into the unknown. Past human contacts were severed understandably, and not likely to ever be renewed.

Kronkite called Starfarer whenever the satellite contact could be made.

"One thing good about space travel," said Atom, "we're not bothered getting phony scam calls. What is Sara doing nowadays, Kronkite?"

"She's conducting a new comparative study on the difference between goal-oriented people and those without goals. Of course, she's already pointed to me as a *goal* extremist. Over."

Atom and Evelyn smiled. "Sounds like she's pegged you right," said Evelyn. "We'd like to see that study. By the way, we can't thank you enough for the writings you micro-chipped to us. There's a lot of meat in 'em, even for a vegetarian like me."

"Yeah," said Atom "The subject's given us a lot to chew on."

Kronkite laughed. "Glad to find you in good spirits. I think now I should have added *humor* to my virtues list. Humor is very important in life. Seriously, let me tell you, you both rank very high on that list, and I thank you for that."

"I think you believe in us more than we believe in ourselves," said

99

Evelyn.

"Believe in yourself! As I believe in you wholeheartedly," said Kronkite.

"We appreciate your faith in us, but sometimes I don't think I know enough," said Atom.

"I know what you mean," said Kronkite. "We're finite and knowledge is infinite. I know I will never know everything there is to know. When it's needed, it finds me. Knowledge comes best with experience and integrity. That's all I can say."

"One thing I *do* know— it's not found in old books." said Evelyn. "We've found that very old books are poor guides for life or health. Many are full of fables that are... more foible than fact."

Kronkite laughed. "Evelyn, you're as clever with words as you are with plants. You're a keeper."

"We really enjoy our conversations with you, Kronkite," said Atom.

"Yes," agreed Evelyn.

"I enjoy our talks, too," said Kronkite. "Many great ideas come from talking. Our speech is one of the advantages we have over other species."

Suddenly, the speaker crackled hissing static.

"What's...*buzz, zzzt*...that?" asked Kronkite. "Ov..."

"What? What'd he say? We must be losing our transmission."

"Yah...*zzzt*...tawk...ta...mor-r-r-rr-...owt..." *Buzz hiss-s-s...zzt...*

"We lost him for today," said Atom. Must've rotated out of range. We'll try again tomorrow."

With no planets to vary the journey, Starfarer sped on through the monotony of space. The four astronauts fell into their respective routines, performing their duties mechanically like soldiers or automatons. Each day became a summary of the day before and the day after that.

Orwell maintained and oversaw the spaceship equipment. Darla was attached to her radio and ROSS scanning. Evelyn managed the greenhouse with much skill and dedication. Atom kept a log of their progress. The cross-training that had initially begun, was largely abandoned. Each performed his or her duties routinely, and mostly unaided. The scheduled regularity helped fill their time.

Meals, movies, and, especially, calls from Kronkite or Sara provided most of the diversion. Relations between the couples and each other were stable.

There was something sobering about space. The bigger it loomed in the mind, the more the mind sought solace in little things. For Evelyn, it was the elegance of a tiny flower. For Darla, it was her facility with the radio equipment. For Atom, it was logging progress, charting and observing the immense expanse of space. For Orwell, after a minimum of maintenance, it was escape into the fictional realm of adventure movies. Control of life's little aspects obliterated the uncertainty of the astronaut's day to day existence, and especially their future.

Atom met Orwell in the hallway between the library and recreation room. "Have you read Kronkite's code of Virtues and Vices?" Atom asked.

"Kronkite's code?" Orwell replied hazily.

"The compressed microchip I showed you and Darla."

"I looked at it."

"What did you think of it?"

"I didn't."

"How do you mean?"

"Just that."

"You mean, it didn't make sense to you, or you didn't care about it?"

"It could mean something, and it could be rubbish."

"Could you give me an example?" Atom asked.

Orwell thought for a moment. "Okay, what about envy— envy and lust?"

Atom was surprised by the question. His first impression had been that Orwell had not examined the code. The thrust of the question on envy and lust, however, seemed to indicate that Orwell had given considerable thought to it.

"When you talked with Kronkite on your last radio time, did you discuss your questions with him?"

"Not exactly. That's too much like me talking to my old man. I never discussed things with him either. He was kind of inept, tried to live through me, I think. Anyway, I was always one step ahead of him. As for Kronkite? True, he's a great inventor and all that, but those ideas of his...I don't think much of 'em. They're too abstract, you know what I mean? How are you going to apply 'em? It's all dreamland stuff."

Atom had only brought up the subject in a light general manner, expecting to hear a casual comment of interest or approval. He wasn't prepared for a deeper discussion on the topic. But, since he was interested, he decided to pursue it anyway. It wasn't often he had conversations with Orwell. Usually they left him with a vague feeling of discontent. Still, he hungered for the companionship. At the same time, he didn't want to raise Orwell's ire. He dreaded Orwell's moody backlashes. It was sort of like stroking a pet and having it snap at you.

"You must have given it some thought where envy and lust would fit into the avoid list?"

"Yeah, I did and I didn't find 'em there. I could probably come up with a better list than Kronkite. This is my off-time. See you later." Orwell walked off to the recreation room, and closed the door after him.

Atom opened the library door, and entered the control room. Darla was at the radio console.

"Hi," she said as he entered.

"Putting in some extra ROSS time scanning again, are you?"

"Yes," said Darla. "I get restless. This is like opening strange cabinet doors and wondering what I'll find inside. Who knows? Maybe I'll find something and be surprised. Mostly I find nothing. It reminds me of when our family used to drive through the mountains and we couldn't find a decent radio station. Right now, any sound, except for static, any strange noise would make me happy."

Darla tried some different frequencies. "Are we halfway yet?"

Atom looked at the screen, as if that could answer the question. "No, hardly," he sighed heavily. "Our speed isn't what it should be, either. I can't figure it out. We can't be bucking a headwind," he said. "Maybe it's my imagination, or I'm too impatient."

Atom sat down with his charts and studied them. Darla came over and put her hand on his arm and looked over his shoulder.

"This whole configuration of nebulae is arrayed in a giant curved pattern. The whole system is rushing toward us very rapidly, so that should cut our travel time in more than half. Besides, without resistance of gravity or air friction, we're traveling at a fantastic speed. Reaching another galaxy would be impossible otherwise. Still, it's a mighty distance to travel."

Astronomers surmise that this interstellar space is a complete void. No one has ever mapped it, however. There may be forces we know nothing about."

"Dangers, you mean?" said Darla. "Like worm holes, black holes, or dark matter?"

"Precisely. I wish I could answer that with assurance, Darla, but my answer would blow up a Verity Scanner. I am relieved that I haven't seen any obstruction yet at the center of this ocean of space. Nor is there an indication of any anomaly or black hole that we could be sucked into. There may be currents that I'm not aware of that could slow our progress, though.

"That wouldn't be good, would it?" asked Darla.

"No. It would mean more travel years and maybe deplete our fuel entirely."

Darla understood the implications, but didn't allow herself to voice them. The thought of drifting forever in space was just too oppressive for words.

"I'm changing our course to see if I can get out of the slight doldrums that we're in. I hate to do it, because it puts us off course for our targeted galaxy. It might also mean we'd have to select a different galaxy altogether.

However, that's not a very viable option."

Later in their scheduled afternoon, Atom and Evelyn went to the control room for their daily chat with Kronkite. The sound quality was abominable. It was painful to listen. The crackling erected a barrier to their talk. Yet, they persisted. It was like trying to read a letter in scrawly, illegible handwriting. If you wanted the message badly enough, you'd keep at it.

"What did you say?" asked Kronkite. "You're experiencing resistance? Over."

"Yes, Starfarer is losing some momentum," said Atom. He shouted as if Kronkite was in the next room. And by shouting loud enough, he might be heard better.

"Couldn't quite get that. Existent, what?" Kronkite struggled to understand Atom.

"No. Re...sis...tance!" Atom emphasized. "It's like a wall...a wall in our way. This is different than the astronomers had predicted for us. Over."

"Resistance? You're in a better position to appraise it than we are. Of course, the astronomers will want to hear about...*zzt*...it. I'll consult with...with...*zzt* the staff experts...*zzt*...today. Moreover...*zzt*... *zzt-zzzt...crackle...!*

Atom and Evelyn tried to resume radio contact, despite the fact that they knew time was up. They had lost the transmission window till the next rotation.

"Did you understand his last words? I couldn't separate the last sentence from the static," said Atom with the irritation one feels from frustration.

Evelyn shook her head. "It'll have to wait till tomorrow. He'll undoubtedly confer with the staff astronomers and have some explanation to give you. How about taking a walk? I'm cramped from being glued to the speakers."

"Good idea, sweetheart. It's been awhile since we had a good stroll. Atom and Evelyn left the control room walking hand-in-hand.

CHAPTER XXI

There are many key moments in life. Many moments that constitute pegs to attach memories. Conception is a key moment. It's a totally involved moment. But it is lacking in conscious knowledge by the individual conceived. The father and the mother are the conscious perpetrators. Even then, their role is limited as any infertile couples or unwary teenagers can attest. The sperm are the active participants. But no result is possible without the egg and proper timing. Key moments only exist when they are timely.

Birth constitutes another peg. The officiators— mainly the mother— are the conscious witnesses of the event. The newborn, although having a central role in the drama, again is without the requisite consciousness of it. All of this accounts for the scarcity of autobiographies of sperm, fetuses, or newborns. Look at your baby pictures. That was you. Do you remember yourself as a baby? You were active. You cried. You gooed. You drooled. You wet. Every bit of you was there, except not much consciousness as yet. So many key moments during all those months, but hardly a one remains to hang a peg of remembrance.

Kindergarten. Do you remember that peg? What about first or second grade? Third, fourth, fifth, sixth, seventh, or eighth? Do you remember all your teacher's names? Do you remember all your tests, assignments, and grades? Why not? You lived them.

Other memory pegs include: vacations, outings, travel, homes, streets, stores, games, hobbies, graduations, illnesses, injuries, pain, parents, siblings, relatives, friends, lovers, tormentors, marriages, partings, divorces, successes, failures, defeats, losses, separations, deaths; all pegs for remembrance.

Adult life, less limited, contains many pegs that evoke memories. Many more pegs than childhood. One wonders why. Perhaps it's the arrival of that condition called consciousness.

Even adult life is limited in the number of pegs it retains, the number of memories that can be revived. What was her name? Who was he? When was that? Where did I put that? Many desired recollections evade us.

It seems that emotional content contributes something to hammering in pegs, making them secure on the wall of life. That's the wall which you

104

hang the family portraits on. Also, the same wall on which you hang your diplomas and your vacation pictures. Emotion seems to have a significant role in establishing long-term memories. What role that is would be a subject for Sara.

Kronkite's life was full of normal and exceptional pegs. He was about to acquire another.

The day following his discussion with Atom, Kronkite summoned his staff of astronomy experts. Starfarer was losing velocity. There was some resistance to its progress.

The men and women on the staff were among the most distinguished and renowned in astronomy. Their credentials were impeccable, their reputations were sterling, their acclaim was prestigious. In short, they were authoritative and reliable. The group of four met around the conference table at the Space Center. At Kronkite's elbow was a chart, a flat representation of the multidimensional entity — *cosmic space.*

"Starfarer is located approximately here," said Kronkite pointing to a location on the chart. "They have long since left the orbiting path of the last planet of our solar system. I think we can safely rule out the exertion of any gravitational pull from any nearby bodies, do you agree?"

Brampton, a ruddy-complexioned man in a rumpled tweed jacket was first of the astronomers to speak. He was careless of dress and appearance, but consumed with the cosmos. "There is a belt of asteroids adjacent. Collectively, they might produce an effect that we're unaware of. Neither of them, however, should cause the effect you mention."

"Yes, I agree," said Maureen. In contrast to Brampton, she was faultlessly dressed. She had a smooth, moon-shaped face with an upswept hairdo.

The third astronomer, Garth, was dressed in a lab jacket with a pocketful of pens. He was a quiet, studious man, a copious note-taker, and a nodder.

"Is that the consensus, then?" asked Kronkite.

Garth nodded.

"In our observation, matter is minute in comparison to space. Yet matter gets most of our attention. Even then, in the cataloging of it, we've only just begun. Our century of photographic observation is minuscule in comparison to cosmic eternity. Relatively speaking, we are dealing with a split second, whereas, the cosmos runs on eon time. What I'm getting at is this: our best knowledge of space is limited to the troposphere, stratosphere, and ionosphere. We tend to lump all the rest of outer space into one category. Space may possibly have more regions than even our imagination allows. We may be seeing the trees and ignoring the forest."

"Yes, I see what you're driving at," said Maureen. "There is a danger that we fix our attention too much on solid matter. And I would add this. There may be invisible gases, bands of magnetic force, currents like solar winds that our radio and telescopic instruments don't pick up."

Garth nodded.

"From what Starfarer is reporting, we may have to revise our thinking about outer space entirely. It may prove to be as complex a system as our oceans, with their tides, streams, and underwater currents."

Garth again nodded.

"What advice can I give Atom?" asked Kronkite. "He's out there with limited resources, far from help, if this problem can't be solved. The Starfarer expedition could be stalled in space forever."

Garth looked helplessly at Brampton and then at Maureen.

"I wish we could help them," said Brampton. "As far as the condition they are experiencing, we are the distant observers. The astronauts are closer to the answer than we here can ever be. Ours can only be a speculation from afar, while they can make decisions based upon on-the-spot observations. At this point, the knowledge they're acquiring is far more valuable and real than any of our remote sightings could ever be. I envy them for that."

"Which puts us back to where we started. They're left almost totally to fend for themselves," said Kronkite with a tinge of frustration in his voice.

"I'd say so, yes," concluded Brampton. "Theories are fine for discussion, but also dangerous when not grounded on any factual content. We are not in a position to give them the knowledge they need. They are. The astronauts must deal with the real and the practical that they find out there. I would say that that is their only course of action."

Maureen and Garth both nodded.

That evening at radio time, Kronkite paced the floor as Ames sat at the console.

When the time arrived, they began calling.

"Kronkite calling Starfarer. Over"

A static hiss was heard. Then a faint sound of a voice.

"This is Atom. I can barely hear you. Speak slowly. Maybe I can understand you. Over"

"Atom, I met with experts. They suggested the possibility of a magnetic field or current...*crackle...zzt... hiss....*"

"Repeat, please. I couldn't make out what you said, Kronkite. Over."
crackle...crackle...

"Check the...*zzt...zzzt...*fields"... *crackle...zzt....*

"We're losing your transmission." *crackle...zzt...zzt.........*

*   *   *

106

Back at ground control Kronkite and Ames stared helplessly at the radio receiver.

"Atom, can you hear me? Atom...Atom...Atom!"

"Better tell him we'll try tomorrow," said Ames.

The speaker crackled and hissed. He tried again with the same result. Ames gave the switch a final flick. Kronkite stared at the console. Then he pivoted in his chair and shakily stood up and walked out, leaving the center. Sara was in the parking lot waiting for him. She could see that he was dejected.

"We're losing radio contact," he said, his voice breaking.

The next day, and days after, he tried calling at the most effective radio time with no success.

After that, activity at ground control center slacked off to minimum staffing.

"I've been racking my brain how we could amplify our signal," said Kronkite. "Nothing I've tried gives it any added boost."

"Anything we could send now would never catch up to them," said Ames. "It would always be years behind and too weak. Like everything else, technology has its limits."

"Yeah," said Kronkite, "everything has limits, except the heart. That persists."

Six days later, when Kronkite had finally accepted that establishing radio contact with Starfarer was now hopeless, he booked a vacation cruise for Sara and himself. It was the most happy and most sorrowful vacation of their lives.

The recollection of Atom's voice from Sarfarer's radio was one of those emotional occasions; one of those life pegs on which one hangs a reminiscence of loss.

The Starfarer astronauts were gone forever.

CHAPTER XXII

"Didn't you just watch that movie?" asked Darla, as she joined Orwell in the recreation room. It was a very innocent question meant only to elicit information. Orwell was reclining on what passed for a couch on the spaceship. It had become his most frequent posture. He put the movie on *PAUSE.*

"What else is there to do in this damn box?" he answered, somewhat testily. Then a smile crept across his face. "Of course, we could go up to the pilothouse and fly around like birds and make love."

Darla smiled half-heartedly. She was hoping his smile indicated an upturn in his mood. Since they had left their galaxy and entered the immensity of interstellar space, they had not made love much.

"Why don't we go do some of the exercises?" Darla suggested. "You know how good a workout makes you feel."

"What for? So, I can become a champion athlete? Maybe try out for a team? Maybe I'd have been a sports star; might have been voted MVP."

Darla regretted making her suggestion.

"That's comical, isn't it?" Orwell said ironically. "Me, become a star. Stardom. Or rather, star *dumb*! We don't *have* a star, you know that? Not one *effin* star. Not one! We left *our* star behind. It used to shine on us in the morning, and make sunsets for us at dusk. Now we're way out in the middle of nowhere and can't get to one. All those stars to choose from like cherries on a tree, and we can't reach one. Not one of 'em. Doesn't that just crack you up? All those zillions of tantalizing stars and we can't get to one. Not one of 'em."

Darla tried to sit down by him to provide some comfort. In his annoyance, he didn't make any room for her. He was oblivious to her, and captured by his gloom that ran on non-stop.

"I don't know why I ever signed on for this. The biggest damned mistake I ever made. I threw my life away. For what? To be a hero? To be in the headlines? Have a place in history? That's just ink on paper for a dog to crap on. It was a lousy trade, do you know that, Darla? I shouldn't have let you talk me into it."

"Me?... Talk you...?" The remark stung. Darla's eyes bleared under here eyelids.

"I don't want to talk about it anymore," he said clicking on the movie again. The conversation was effectively over. Darla stood up with tears in her eyes. Orwell made no move to stop her from leaving. She walked back to their bedroom, undressed, and climbed into bed.

Meanwhile, Atom and Evelyn were in the greenhouse. She had brought him with her to show him something. She was very excited.

"Do you remember I told you I had several experiments I wanted to try in the weightless condition of the pilothouse?"

"Yes," he said, tuning in to Evelyn's excitement.

"Well, here it is."

Atom looked at the fruit, but he wasn't sure what he should be seeing.

"This is one of my new hybrids. I did it through grafting. Remember how often I tried this same experiment back home and it never took, and I'd get so discouraged? You always told me not to give up. Well, I didn't."

Atom smiled at his wife and gave her a hug, but he still didn't get it. "Why did it work this time and not before?"

"I can't be positive," Evelyn said, taking a scientist's caution, "but I think doing the graft in the weightless pilothouse did the trick. Since grafting is an artificial process attaching one branch to another, I always had difficulties with the joined parts breaking at the weak point of the graft. The fibers of this plant are naturally quite delicate and rely on their tubular, rather than tensile strength for support. In weightlessness, this is not a problem."

"You're an inspiration," said Atom. "I'd like to tell Kronkite about it. He'd be so proud."

Then Atom felt a heaviness of heart when he thought only two weeks ago, of when he and Kronkite had last talked. He tried calling many times after that, but he was beginning to accept the fact that they would never talk again. It had the finality of death.

Evelyn sensed his sorrow and was quick to comfort him.

"I'm pretty well caught up on my greenhouse work today," she said. "Why don't I spend some time with you in the control room?"

"I'd like that," he said. "Maybe some of your success will rub off on me."

They rode down the can and walked together to the control room. "I was hoping the experts could give me some advice about the seeming resistance we're running into. Either the astronomers didn't know, or there wasn't time for them to tell me. That's a problem for me. With years ahead to reach our destination, we can't afford delay."

Evelyn looked at his chart and then at the screen. She had some understanding of them, but was not acquainted with the navigational aspects. "What is the worst that could happen?" she asked.

"The worst— it's almost happening now— we could become stalled in here. Suspended in the middle of this void. Like being lost in the middle of a big ocean with no hope of rescue."

"Is that the galaxy we're heading for?" asked Evelyn, pointing to a little twinkling spot on the black background on the screen.

"That's it."

"So many celestial bodies out there, and all so far apart. It never ceases to amaze me." Evelyn shook her head. "Are they all quite similar, do you think?"

"We won't know until we get there. I suppose they have certain similarities like your plants," said Atom. "Except they'll have enough differences to make a difference to us."

"To me, my plants are all individuals; quite different, each one."

"Well, to you, yes. I can see why you'd think that. You study them so closely. For you, there would be as many differences as there are fingerprints, I suppose. Yet they're certainly not as uncountable as the stars," said Atom, pointing at the glittering array of galaxies on the screen.

"That is an interesting question. Back home, there were about 250,000 different plant varieties. And all of them weren't cataloged. If there are other planets with plants— as I hope there are— that could add up to a lot more."

"I hope there are, sweetheart. For your sake and mine," said Atom.

He studied his chart again. He was worried, far more worried than he admitted to Evelyn. He desperately needed to talk to someone about the situation. However, he didn't want to worry her, too.

Just then, the control room door opened. Orwell entered, taking a quick glance around.

"Oh, I thought Darla might be here," he said. "She spends so much time at that damn ROSS scanner. Sometimes I think she spends more time with that damn thing than me. Have you seen her?"

"No," said Evelyn. "She hasn't been in here. Not since we arrived, anyway. Did *you* see her, Atom?"

Atom shook his head.

"That's just like her. Does as she damn well pleases, doesn't she? Here we are, crammed into this crappy spaceship, and I can't even find her. She can't very well run away on me, can she?"

Orwell had gotten in the habit of making statements in the form of questions. The questions didn't invite anyone's response.

"Checking the charts again, are you? Tell me. Level with me. It's been over three and a half years. Are we on schedule or not?" Over time, Orwell had matured from a young enthusiast into an acerbic cynic. It was not a pleasant transformation.

110

"We're not where I'd like us to be," admitted Atom. He dreaded the question from Orwell. However, he knew it couldn't be avoided. All of their lives were involved. There was no concealing the problem.

"Why don't you say it?" said Orwell. "We're not making it are we? Not making it."

"You haven't given up hope, have you?"

"You mean living optimism, endurance, practicing friendship, and all that other Kronkite crap? That's all boy scout stuff." Orwell left the control room in a huff.

Atom and Evelyn looked at each other and sighed. The problem with Starfarer's progress was bad enough without the extra burden of Orwell's whining and tantrums to cope with.

"What am I to do?" groaned Atom, crouched over his chart, head in hands. "Things are bad enough, without Orwell making them worse?"

Evelyn was thinking, but no solutions were forthcoming. She thought of her plants— how placid and peaceful they were, compared to all this turmoil. She wanted to contribute something to solve the problem, but she couldn't think what that would be. At least, she could retreat to her greenhouse for peace of mind. "I can't think what to suggest, sweetheart. This just seems to be a repeat of the other time Orwell became so despondent. Maybe it'll pass of its own accord."

"If only it was his shifting moods we had to deal with," said Atom. "We're losing more and more progress every day."

111

CHAPTER XXIII

Darla began spending more time in the control room with Atom. Ostensibly, it was to use the ROSS scanner. Atom, always working on navigation charts, provided much needed companionship when Orwell was in one of his cranky moods.

"Get any signals today?" Atom asked.

"No, but I'm going to keep trying. Back home, radio operators were concerned with noise pollution. Out here, I'm overwhelmed with silence. Paradoxical, isn't it?"

"Sure is."

"Will you teach me some more about charting today?"

"Sure, why not?" said Atom, sliding over to make room for her beside him.

Darla sat by Atom with all the rapt attention of a moonstruck teacher's pet.

"You're very spring-like today," he said.

"Really? Why do you think so?" giving Atom a demure look.

"You just strike me as being spring fresh for some reason. If I'm not mistaken, I detect a whiff of perfume about you. Fragrances have a way of stimulating memories in me. I don't know why."

"Yes, that happens to me, too. I don't know what season it would be back home. I've lost track."

"Me, too. It doesn't seem to matter anymore."

"I still remember one of the most pleasant talks I had with Kronkite and Sara. They had gone on a picnic at Rainbow Lake. I used to swim there as a kid. It had a great beach."

"Sounds nice."

"Yeah, it was. And you know what?"

"What?" Atom smiled and chuckled to himself. "Kronkite skipped a stone in the lake for me. It skipped six times, I think he said."

"That sounds like fun. Kronkite and Sara were wonderful people and a wonderful couple. There was something special about their relationship. I always wanted to be— you know— in love the way they were," said Darla.

"It wasn't all perfect. Not even with Kronkite. He was a pretty hard-working guy. I guess most would call him a workaholic. I wonder if Sara

112

ever got that vacation he promised her."

"Knowing her," said Darla," she did. She managed Kronkite pretty effectively in her own sweet, psychological way. She knew better ways than nagging."

"Yes. But more important, I think they genuinely respected each other, and were nurturing of each other's careers."

"And loved each other, wouldn't you say?"

"Yes, they were definitely on the same wave-length."

"Why, Atom, that sounds like radio talk," said Darla.

"Let's get to the navigation, before you get me drawn into your field."

"If you say so," smiled Darla.

"Yes, I think so. One *sparks* on a spaceship ought to be enough. Two might be a crowd. So on with the navigation lesson. Now, here's the log. Note here is our daily progress."

Darla studied the logbook carefully. The numbers seem to be decreasing. Is that good?"

"I'm afraid not."

"Why?"

"We're not making the progress I was hoping for. There's nothing in this void to give us a gravity assist. I don't mind telling you, I'm concerned."

"What can you do about it?"

"Frankly, so far there isn't much I *can* do. However, I have a plan to redirect our course. I may have to redirect the auto-pilot controls as well from our present course."

"And if that doesn't work?"

"I'd rather not think about that possibility just now. So much is riding on it. I'm going to meet Evelyn for our break. Want to join us?"

"No, I think I'll stay on here. I may try a few more ROSS scans before I turn in. Would you stop by my room when you're done with your break? I have something for you."

"Can't it wait until tomorrow?" asked Atom.

"It could, but— why don't you stop by anyway? You'll be going right by, anyhow."

"Yes, all right."

A few minutes later, Atom joined Evelyn in the lab. She was doing some plant analysis with the electron microscope.

"What are you working on today, sweetheart?" asked Atom.

"I've been studying the cellular structure of some of my climbing plants."

"Yes, I remember you telling me about that. I suggested you send them to a climbing school. Most people like to think more schooling will solve problems. And you said it never does. Real thinking is more beneficial."

Evelyn laughed. "Yes. And thinking about my problem, it suddenly dawned on me— it's so ridiculously simple, I'm ashamed of myself."

"Oh, why?"

"Call it simplistic thinking. I was grafting— pardon my pun— animal skills onto my plants. It was almost like how savages imagined stone statues were somehow alive; somehow could produce miracles. You can probably guess what I'm driving at."

"No," said Atom. "I think you're driving up a hill, and not letting me see what's ahead."

"It's obvious. The stationary lights in the greenhouse don't assist the tendrils in spiraling like the sun does. The tendrils don't operate like muscles. They're light-seeking. Therefore, what I need is a movable light source to simulate planet movement. Get it?" said Evelyn.

"Sweetheart, you never cease to amaze me."

"Orwell is coming later to the greenhouse. We're going to see if we can't simulate sunshine movement as a plant might see it. The light won't have to move actually. Having them turn on and off in a directional pattern, we hope to suggest the movement. Orwell says he can do it with a relay switching device."

"I hope it all works out. Knowing you, I'm sure it will. See you later," said Atom.

A short while later, Orwell joined Evelyn in the greenhouse. They began adjusting the lights and attaching them to a series of switching relays."

"Are you as aware of other things as you are of your plants?" asked Orwell.

Evelyn looked at Orwell, puzzled by his question. "What do you mean?" She asked.

"I mean, like a banker will spot a counterfeit bill quicker than an ordinary person, because he's alert to it."

"I'm sorry, but I just don't know what you're driving at," said Evelyn.

"I guess I just gotta lay it all out for you, then, huh?"

"Yes, I think you'll have to."

Orwell paused and took a deep breath. He looked at Evelyn with a penetrating gaze before he spoke. "Your husband...he's having an affair with my wife."

Evelyn was struck so speechless by Orwell's accusation, that she forgot all about her plants, the lights, everything.

"You must have had some inkling," he said. "It's been going on for quite some time."

"No, I..."

"You mean to say, you haven't noticed all the time they spend together while you're down here in the greenhouse?"

"Well, I know they work together in the control room, but…"

"Now, maybe you'll understand what's been on my mind of late. I can't keep quiet about it any longer. It isn't right. That's why I had to tell you about it."

"I don't know…," said Evelyn.

"I do. Understand, I'm not blaming it all on him. She's to blame, too."

"How do you know?"

"I've seen 'em. That's how I know. I don't expect you to take my word for it. Keep an eye on 'em yourself. Then you'll know."

Orwell left the greenhouse as darkly as he'd come.

In the meantime, Atom knocked on Darla's door. She greeted him in her form-fitting silk nightie.

"Oh, pardon me. I didn't know you were getting ready for bed."

"That's okay. I'm glad you stopped by," she said. This will only take a minute."

Atom walked in. He was surprised by her near nakedness. She had always been so modest and reticent in the past.

"I have something I want to give you." She reached over among her collection of keepsakes and picked out a little two-inch plastic bear. She came right up to Atom and slipped the toy bear into his coat pocket. The tiny plastic souvenir bear had an inscription on it which read *I'd BEAR anything for you!*

She gave Atom a little kiss on the cheek. "That's for being such a good teacher," she said. "It's my lucky bear. I hope it brings you good luck, too."

Atom couldn't help thinking what a girlish thing she had done. It was a foolish little memento. So, what? If it pleased her, what was the harm? He walked to the door and she saw him out.

"Smiling, she stood waving in her short nightie as Atom walked up the hallway.

Approaching the hall from the other direction was Evelyn. She saw Atom disappear up the hallway. She saw Darla waving after him. Darla saw Evelyn and, somewhat guiltily and embarrassed, closed her door without a word.

CHAPTER XXIV

There are moments in time when events so converge, that collision is inevitable. Fortunately, space is immense and permits a high degree of maneuverability. The vast expanse of space allows for multiple choices. It permits numerous bodies to have room in which to rest, to move, and to act.

The bodies in space differ in force, mass, and nature. Some of them are solid, some icy, some fiery, some kinetic, some misty, some explosive. The interplay between these bodies create different and, many times, unpredictable effects. Reaction may start small at a distance, grow in proximity and can be catastrophic in collision.

Such a collision was approaching aboard the spaceship, Starfarer.

Bodies too narrowly confined in space, bodies whose paths often interact, bodies whose direction is inflexibly set, are more likely to collide. All three conditions existed on Starfarer.

Added to this matter was volition. The effect of mind moving matter with passion, desire, hurt, fear, anger, hostility, and jealousy.

They had reached the midway point of their journey. There was definitely no turning back. And there was little prospect of hurrying their progress. So far as is known, matter moves methodically while mind alone feels impatience with movement. A comet traversing space is content to go from point A to point B with no annoyance with the allotted time. The difference between the comet that moves, and the mind that feels, may be that the comet is unaware of its future demise.

The astronauts were aware of their time element in space travel. They were not fully aware, however, of the effect it would have on them, particularly when they were faced with unforeseen delay.

It was like signing a contract and being unhappy with the time payments. Minds are subject to change. One may grow to regret a debt contracted too early, and for too extended a period of time.

The four astronauts had signed on to Starfarer in good faith. They were honest and intelligent and knew their own minds, at least as well as any young, inexperienced minds can know themselves.

Travel always has an appealing element of adventure to it, which cloaks the inconvenience one is likely to encounter. There's something

116

very gratifying about new scenery that delights the mind. It would be interesting to see how a travel agent would promote the Starfarer trip in a brochure.

The final destination must be what girds the pioneer or migrant to the hardship of his journey. Otherwise, most everyone would stay home. This element in the Starfarer project was hazy at best. Then there are those few individuals who love adventure, who want to be first at something or who, for some reason or other, are discontent with their present circumstances.

Orwell fit the former categories, and Atom more the latter. A few women also have the above natures, but once coupled with a man, they tend to join his enterprise. Bonding, family, and the nesting instinct may have something to do with it. Whatever the migration or enterprise, the inherent danger of it seems to have little effect on women. They are as willing to accept the risk of any undertaking as the men. Maybe it's instinctive. *Something* about the sympathetic part of a woman's nature makes her particularly vulnerable to abusers and scoundrels. Even when convicted and incarcerated, the most vicious killer can expect to find some attentive female.

Atom and Orwell did not have vicious natures. In a large population, their temperaments would have fallen into the middle. Regardless, similar temperaments can come into conflict. Evelyn and Darla were women with large sympathies. They would also register in the middle of any population. Neither was excessively possessive or promiscuous. Nevertheless, similar women can be in conflict, also.

Darla and Atom continued to spend a lot of time together in the control room. He, fastidiously making calculations and charts. She, monitoring the ROSS scanner and learning about space navigation.

There was an undercurrent aboard the Starfarer of which neither Atom or Darla were aware.

One day, during his duty time, Atom decided to go up to the pilothouse to make some sightings through the windows, rather than from the surveillance screen. Outside was as dark as night, except for the tiny distant cosmic stars.

Darla was on her recreation time and decided to join him. One by one, they rode "the can" up to the pilot house. The astronauts didn't spend much time in the weightlessness of the pilot room. There was no particular reason for that, other than it was sort of a nuisance to ride the tubular elevator up.

In some respects, it was like leaving a house and going out on a balcony. There were no window views in their living compartments. The centrifugal gravity compartments had only video screen views.

It was strange to float weightless again after such a lapse of time.

"I'd almost forgotten what it was like in here," Darla said.

"Me, too," Atom said looking at all with renewed interest. "There's one thing about looking for long periods at a monitor screen that jades the sense of— I almost said the real world— I should have said the cosmos."

Atom and Darla settled lightly into the front launch seats and loosely buckled the straps. In front of them was space. Space with a capital 'S'. Space with its myriads of spiraling, sparkling nebulae.

"Maybe this will give me a fresh outlook on the problem. At least, I hope it will. I remember back home getting stuck on a school assignment, and I'd take a walk outside. Not to see anything in particular. Just for the change. I always found that it cleared my thinking somehow. I can't explain why.

Sometimes I find that if I stare at something too close, for too long a time, I can't see it at all anymore."

"I wish I could help you on it," said Darla. "I'm beginning to get a feel for how you make the calculations. You've been an excellent instructor on that. It seems like navigating such distances, you can't really affect anything."

"Strange, that's how I've felt for a long time. It's like being a minnow crossing an ocean. I haven't given up, but nevertheless, it gets me down sometimes. I feel overwhelmed by the distance. Yet, I've got to keep swimming on as though we have forever, that the end of time doesn't exist."

Atom pointed out the window. "See that twinkling star? That little dot of punctuation is our destination, if we can ever get there. The cosmos is moving to meet us, and we're rushing to meet it at an extremely fast speed— a speed that we're largely insensible of— a speed that would have gotten us a speeding ticket back home. Oh, but it takes such a long time to get there and then...."

"We'll get there," said Darla. "I'm confident we will."

"When you think of it, Darla, this view is astonishing. What wouldn't any astronomer back home give to be in our place right now?" Just then, they heard the tube elevator being summoned back. Atom and Darla looked at each other. "Wonder who's coming up."

Orwell came flying into the pilot cabin!

"So, this is where you're hiding? I've been looking everywhere for you," Orwell ranted, fiercely scowling.

Atom and Darla turned to look at him. Orwell was in a rage and completely out of control.

He flew at Atom with his arms flailing. He was trying to inflict injury on Atom any way he could. His momentum carried his feet to the ceiling. Darla shielded her face with her arms and tried to cry out, but nothing came.

"You gotta be the big mucky-muck and steal my woman, you bastard!" Orwell yelled incoherently.

Orwell cartwheeled over the seat crashing into the window frame. Darla unbuckled and fled to the elevator. She didn't have the slightest notion of what she could do. There was no reasoning with Orwell's wrath. Perhaps Orwell would follow her and that would break up the fight.

What if he attacked her— attempted to murder her? In his present state, she had no idea what he was capable of. She made it to "the can" and sped down into the gallery. Was her husband going to follow her? She would have to hide or— Evelyn? Where was she? Darla really didn't know how Evelyn could help. It was better than doing nothing. Perhaps together they could think of something to stop the fight.

Darla raced through the passageway calling out, "Evelyn! Evelyn!"

Evelyn, in the greenhouse tending plants, heard the calls and looked up as Darla rushed in.

"Orwell is attacking Atom! We've got to stop him!" shrieked Darla, agitated and breathless.

Evelyn was holding a trowel. She dropped it and went with Darla.

"How did it start?" Evelyn asked, her jaw muscles knotting.

"Orwell just came on a rampage into the pilothouse."

They walked hurriedly through the hallway.

"This is all your fault," said Evelyn.

Darla looked at Evelyn in astonishment as they rushed toward the tube elevator together.

Darla could only say, "What?"

"You heard me."

"I don't know what you mean?" said Darla, still trying to catch her breath.

"It's been festering long enough. I think it's good that it's finally out in the open."

At that instant, the shrill whine of the radar warning sounded. It was a non-stop squeal. Just as suddenly, Starfarer lurched, sending Evelyn and Darla tumbling against the wall.

"What was that?" said Evelyn loudly as she tried to maintain her balance.

Darla had been thrown to the floor. "I don't know. Everything's gone mad!"

CHAPTER XXV

Malice always tends to erupt. Its conviction of martyrdom explodes into despicable action. It scorns reason, disdains cost, desires vengeance, and, inevitably, it resorts to violence.

Orwell harbored envy and resentment coupled with the belief that he had been betrayed by Darla and Atom. He was silent about it. It had gnawed at him. He could contain it no longer. It was not a matter of good or bad. It was a matter of burning in the heart. It was pain stoked by powerlessness and suspicion— two deadly forces.

As always, for those who sidestep responsibility and turn to blame, his ire became focused on a scapegoat. In this case, Atom.

Perhaps it was justified. That remained to be seen. Was there an affair going on between Atom and Darla? Raving, storming, Orwell repeatedly flew across the pilot room at Atom— punching and pummeling him.

Atom warded him off as best he could. "Hold on, Orwell! Let's reason this out," said Atom, defending himself by ducking the blows hurled at him.

Orwell continued grappling. His fury was boundless, fed by the energy of his suppressed anger.

There was no Kronkite to intercede this time, no Sara to smooth things out.

Luckily for Atom, the effect of weightlessness was to diminish the force of Orwell's punches. Unfortunately, the futility of his assaults only increased his fury. As a result, he redoubled his efforts, which caused him to further career and ricochet around the cabin.

Had a promoter back home witnessed the fracas, he might have been tempted to invent a new sport— weightless wrestling— with combatants like the Asteroid Assassin verses the Meteor Mauler. Devising such an exhibition ring and putting it in an arena would be a problem, however.

What was happening to Atom was not an exhibition. It was in deadly earnest.

The struggling, twisting, tumbling continued and it seemed it would go on without abate. As in such a conflict, there was no rational means for ending it. The only remedies that seemed available were injury, fatigue, restraint, or death.

Just at that instant, to further complicate matters, the radar siren sounded. It warned of an impending collision. It was loud and it was shrill and it got their attention.

Acting on reflex from their months of training back at Kronkite's Institute, they both fixed their eyes on the radar screen. Slightly to the left of center, a blip appeared and was growing rapidly. Something was fast approaching them out in space. Something that threatened to collide with Starfarer and destroy them all.

As terrifying as that prospect was, it was a welcome respite from the combat. Orwell immediately buckled himself to the seat next to Atom. The unknown object was swiftly bearing down on them. At its tremendous velocity, there was no time for calculation— only instinct and action. Dodge it or be annihilated!

"Hard throttle, right rocket!" commanded Atom.

Orwell acted promptly.

Now, looking through the window, they could see the object of the radar. It was gigantic! A huge comet— hard, stony, metallic-looking, shedding crystals in its wake. They had no hope of surviving a collision with it. Even in weightless space, there would be no contest.

They held their breath. Their muscles tensed imagining the crushing force ahead. The comet was close enough now to see it in all its dreadful detail. Had they been able to observe it in safety, it would have been a magnificent sight. Now, it only affected them with fear and foreboding. It bore down on them like a train, and they were tied to its track!

The rocket blast jostled the astronauts. Atom and Orwell felt its force in the pull on their seat belts. Down below in the passageway, Darla and Evelyn bounced off the wall until they could attach themselves to emergency restraints.

Icy crystals of the comet's bifurcated tail raked Starfarer's hull.

They were two interstellar travelers passing in the night of space. The odds of their meeting was like the chance of being struck by lightning. Nonetheless, rare as it is, lightning does strike.

Atom and Orwell slumped in their seats and let the taut sudden apprehension drain from them.

It was an abrupt moment. A jittery moment. An air-gasping moment.

The tube elevator came up in the pilothouse. Evelyn climbed out.

"What caused that?" she asked immediately. She was not aware of their narrow escape from disaster. She attributed Starfarer's lurch to the fight between the two men. She was not at all in a grateful mood.

"Tell me!" she said angrily. "What's going on?" She was in a temper far different from her usual calm demeanor. Atom pointed to the screen from the aft camera. The heart of her anger quickly subsided. She could see the comet whizzing away from them at breakneck speed.

"We damned near joined forces with that bruiser and headed south," said Atom.

He managed to tease a little smile out of Orwell and a little reduction of anger from Evelyn. It only amounted to temporary relief, however. The former feeling of emotional heaviness in the room was merely derailed momentarily by the comet, not switched off. How they would handle the multiple agendas was a problem as yet unresolved.

"We can be thankful that we survived that mishap. Let's go back down," said Atom.

Atom had some uneasiness as he wondered if they could leave the pilothouse peacefully, since they could only leave in "the can" one at a time. Evelyn left first. Atom watched warily, wondering if Orwell would resume his former pugnacity. No words were exchanged.   Waiting between trips was silent and awkward. Orwell rode down next.

Darla was waiting for them in the main gallery. Evelyn explained to her about the near collision with the comet. They stood together, but were lonely islands.

"Why don't we all go to the dining room and take a break," said Atom.

"No!" Orwell said firmly. "You're not going to get out of it *that* easy, just cuz of that comet. Neither of you."

"Then what do you suggest?" said Atom quietly, but with authority.

"Whatever the cost, let's have it out," continued Orwell.

"Fine. Fine with me," said Atom.

The four stood in the middle of the gallery.

"We're all rational enough, I believe, to carry on this discussion in a more comfortable setting than here. Somewhere we can all sit down. Therefore, I suggest, if it meets with your approval, let's adjourn to the control room. Since we were thrown off course by the comet. I have a few corrections to make to get back on course, and then we can begin."

While Atom made the necessary adjustments to Starfarer's autopilot, the others sat silent and apart like observers waiting for an execution. Orwell had lost his impetuosity, but he remained sullen.

For some reason, Kronkite's words flashed into Atom's mind. What was happening? Early in the journey, it seemed they had followed his virtues well. Or had they? Were they all losing their endurance for the expedition? What about friendship and optimism? Something had gone terribly wrong. Atom mulled over what Kronkite might have recommended. No solution came.

Had they committed one of the seven vices his mentor had warned him about? Which one could it be? Atom recalled Orwell saying something about envy and lust not being on the list. What had he meant by that? What was causing Orwell's angry outburst? None of the categories seemed to fit the situation. Kronkite's words left as quickly as they had flashed across Atom's mind. He put down his navigation instruments and turned to face the others.

"Well, Starfarer is back on course. Now, what about us?" said Atom, looking at each in turn.

"You stole my wife," blurted out a brooding Orwell. "You've been having an affair with her."

"That's not true," said Atom, denying it instantly,

Darla had a troubled hurt look on her face. Evelyn looked stern and angry.

"It is true," said Orwell. "I've known about it for a long time."

Evelyn wondered to herself how it could have been going on so long, and her not know.

They looked at Darla for some confirmation of guilt.

"Admit it, Darla," said Orwell, giving his wife a withering look. He was winning new confidence with his attacks, and it made him feel stronger, more righteous. It gave him relief somehow.

"It's not true," Darla said tearfully. She felt very hurt by Orwell's accusation.

"We have endured your moodiness for some time now," said Atom, looking at Orwell. "You've got to get it through your head that your suspicions are unfounded. Then maybe we can get back to being friends again."

Atom turned to Evelyn, hoping for some assistance to remedy the situation. He could see that she also was questioning him. It bothered him that she could doubt him. He recognized, however, that she had a right to her feelings, and didn't cast any blame on her.

Finally, Evelyn spoke. "There's one way we can clear this up," she said.

"How?" asked Atom, looking directly at his wife.

"The Verity Scanner."

CHAPTER XXVI

The four astronauts were under a lot of stress. Living aboard a cramped spaceship for several years took a lot out of them. It was like being in a submarine and never coming to the surface. They had traveled farther than anyone from their former world. All that, without relief, time-off, or vacation. They had traveled a great distance, and yet their scenery never changed. It was paradoxical to be a space traveler. Claustrophobia was their state. Perpetual night was their environment.

Adding to their discomfort was the darkness that insidiously engulfed their relationships.

It is hard to live with anxiety created by suspicion. Waking or sleeping, it corrodes emotional health and vitality. It burrows into one's inner life and spoils that which should be fresh, exuberant, and spontaneous. It feeds mold-like until it gnaws and consumes its host. Ultimately it was destroying the inner and outer lives of its victims.

Some suspicions are ill-founded, others are warranted. One must always ask the question: is it the nature of the person to be suspicious, or are the suspicions justified by facts? All hinges on this essential distinction.

If the suspicions are unwarranted, then, unless the person is paranoid, the truth should set matters right. On the other hand, misbehavior that proves suspicions justified, can only be rectified by apology and forgiveness. Without both apology and forgiveness, the matter is never resolved.

The astronauts found themselves in that kind of unresolved conflict. It was a terrible bind. Too often in life, such conflicts simmer on and threaten to flare-up on the slightest provocation. The guilty party lies his way out, only to postpone the final explosion.

The worst part was, the astronauts were in a situation from which there was no escape.

Were Atom and Darla guilty of an indiscretion? This was the issue and this was the suspicion.

They spent a lot of time in the control room. They had numerous opportunities to be unfaithful to their mates. A strong attraction existed between them.

Orwell was sure of their guilt. Evelyn was uncertain and troubled.

"There's one way to clear this up," said Evelyn. "The Verity Scanner."

"There's nothing between us but friendship," protested Atom. "I give you my word."

"Yeah," said Orwell, cynically. "That's not good enough to suit me."

Evelyn didn't say anything.

"This is absurd," said Atom. "Where did you get this idea in the first place?" he asked.

"I have my reasons. I'm not blind, you know."

"Meaning?"

"Meaning, I've caught you two together, too often. One time she was even in your arms."

Evelyn didn't join in the questioning. The thought of Atom leaving Darla's room was burnt into her brain.

Jealousy sees what it suspects.

Most feel a sense of outrage when their honesty is questioned. Atom was no exception. Then, some of Kronkite's words came back to him from that final launch day: "Be patient, be compassionate," Kronkite had said.

"All right," said Atom. "If that's what it takes." There was a great temptation on his part to simply assert his denial and assume the mantle of the injured party, but he resisted it.

Orwell went eagerly to the cabinet and brought out the Verity Scanner. He set it up quickly on the chart table and switched it on.

"Stand together, both of you," said Orwell, gesturing to them with his hand. "Stand in front of the Scanner."

A deep feeling of humiliation came over Darla. It was like being a child again and having her hand caught in the cookie jar. She looked aside. Her breathing was shallow. She felt ashamed. She felt a loss of dignity.

Evelyn sat quite frozen. She felt drained of emotion. She felt listless. She felt like going to the greenhouse and being with her plants, where she could find a sense of contentment and decorum again. The strain of the day had exhausted her store of energy and left her depleted of any reserve.

Atom and Darla stood before the Verity Scanner.

Since it was invented, everyone placed a lot of trust in it. Inventions provide comfort. Inventions entertain us. Inventions check our health. They can also sometimes malfunction. Was one ever known to fail? It took a lot of courage for Atom and Darla to stand and be judged by the Verity Scanner.

"Have you had sex with my wife?" Orwell demanded to know.

It was a very tense moment. It was one of those key moments in life which constitute a peg on which to hang a memory for good or ill.

Orwell watched the Scanner while he waited for Atom to answer.

Evelyn's eyes were averted. She knew that from Orwell's reaction, she would have her answer.

"Have you?" repeated Orwell, with almost demonic glee."

"No," said Atom. "Absolutely not."

Orwell stared at the Scanner, waiting... waiting... waiting... waiting for it to generate a response. The Scanner was silent.

Orwell looked at the connections. He checked the switch. He couldn't believe it. He found it hard to believe. The silence of the Verity Scanner proved their innocence. Suspicion has to be chipped away. It doesn't melt away like snow.

Evelyn threw herself into Atom's arms. Her eyes were well-springs of tears.

Orwell was still hunkered over the Verity Scanner, disbelieving. Darla stood totally crushed by the experience. The physical distance was small, but the emotional distance was huge.

A dreadful silence followed, as deathly quiet as all of space. It's never good to be wrong. To be *found* wrong is worse. To have based all your attitudes, all your responses, all your actions on faulty assumptions is terrible. One's sense of worth sinks to zero. The mind grasps for any straw of esteem on which to stay afloat, while the spirit sinks into the depths of despair.

Orwell could not raise his eyes.

What could one say at that precise instant? When feelings are so overpowering, words are paltry things. So much was required of delicacy at that moment.

Darla was utterly dejected. There was no triumph for her in Orwell's fall. No uplift of joy for her spirit. To be suspected, even wrongfully, was to be demeaned.

Kronkite had said on his recorded message: "Love is only true when freely given." He had not said, though he might have, that jealousy demands love, and that is why it's wrong.

This was the end of a long, protracted episode on the Starfarer journey. It had taken its toll on the astronauts. It was an awkward time. Hopefully, it could be the end of something unhealthy, and offer an opportunity for a new start. Perhaps the beginning of something auspicious.

"We've all lived through considerable stress in these past years," said Atom. "If you regret being here, there's nothing I can do about it."

Orwell was sunk in the depths. And Atom, as leader of the expedition, knew that he must raise him up, not stomp on him while he hung precariously on the brink of his fall.

"Our situation is not hopeless. We do need each other, however. Our lives, success, our very survival, depend on our getting along and cooperating. That's all I ask of you," said Atom.

Orwell and Darla were somber and still.

"All of us have regrets, I'm sure," Atom looked compassionately at Orwell. "Do you regret having signed on? If that's how you feel, you might as well admit it."

Orwell nodded his head.

Darla pressed her clutched hand to her forehead. "He blames me for us being here," she sobbed, her voice quivering. "Orwell, didn't you know I would follow you anywhere?"

Orwell looked pathetic. "I'm sorry, honey...." His eyes were red and watery. "Forgive me— forgive my resentment— I— I was wrong— to take it out on you."

Orwell slowly leaned toward her and extended his hands. He looked at her beseechingly.

Darla raised her hand hesitantly till their hands met halfway. Then they embraced in a flood of tears.

With smiles of relief and pleasure, Evelyn and Atom joined in hugging them.

Starfarer was again on course.

CHAPTER XXVII

Questions, thoughts, and fears must have an open forum for expression. Suppression and censorship are alien to clear thinking and progress. When confrontation occurs among flexible, rational, caring people, it can be beneficial. It may even lead to a new synthesis of harmony, as in the case of the Starfarer astronauts.

Sexual desire is normal and natural. It inspires strong feelings and much artistic expression. Those who attempt in any way, to deny it, ban it, or attach guilt to it, are wrong and doomed to fail. It returns to haunt them in distorted, perverted ways.

Rational people do not attach more importance to sexual desire than it deserves. It is a biological function as basic as eating, drinking, and breathing. Nothing more.

The confrontation with Orwell had improved the cohesiveness of the Starfarer group. Atom had acted with patience, kindness, and fairness. He had not resorted to any argument based on authority. Undoubtedly, Kronkite and Sara would have been proud of him. Consequently, Atom's stature as leader of the expedition grew.

The Verity Scanner had done its wonder in clearing the air of suspicion and hostility occasioned by Orwell's unhappiness and jealousy. Orwell had returned to his old buoyant self, with a much-improved attitude and self-esteem. He had accepted responsibility for being a positive contributing member of the Starfarer group. Atom mused to himself privately how little nuances play such a large part in any outcome. If Orwell's Verity Scanner question had asked, *"was Atom attracted to Darla?"*, a *"no"* answer would have triggered a lie response. Atom loved his wife, but he did find Darla desirable.

Desire is, after all, a natural feeling. It's dishonest to deny it. Procreation is part of the instinct for survival. It's one of life's options. Life is full of them. One cannot think without having options. Without options, there would be no thought at all. Options are merely choices from which to select actions. Hopefully, responsible ones.

The greatly improved congeniality on Starfarer, resulted in a new sense of dedication and acceptance of their precarious situation. Everyone was more diligent about his or her duties. More assistance was offered to

Evelyn. It increased her plant production and experimentation. Atom, more relaxed now, could better concentrate on navigation...and he slept better, too. Darla pursued the ROSS scanner with more intensity. And Orwell took a greater interest in all of the activities of the others. He spent less time watching movies, and more time in the greenhouse assisting Evelyn.

The new spirit of cooperation brought about many gains.

"We've got some news," said Orwell, as the astronauts sat down at their dining table. Orwell had been helping Evelyn on a plant experiment.

"Good news? What is your good news?" asked Atom.

Evelyn smiled. "Over the past months, Orwell and I have been experimenting with light, plant growth, and growth cycles. Orwell has concentrated on the greenhouse lighting. He modified wave frequencies which affected the cycles. As a result, I'm happy to report, we have increased plant growth and the maturity of crops for earlier harvesting.

"That *is* good news," said Atom.

Darla, smiling, cast a proud look at her husband.

"Besides," said Evelyn. "The amazing part of it is, it takes less time, less energy, and delivers an excellent crop. It's just more efficient in every way."

"Wow," said Atom, half in jest, "that's good news alright. Beam me up some of that good stuff."

"As a matter of fact," said Evelyn, "our moods are greatly affected by light rays and we don't know as much about light as we should."

"Yeah, the quality of the light in most of Starfarer is not very good. I know I've felt a lot happier since I've spent more time in the greenhouse," said Orwell. "I can't prove it, but I have felt better."

"Too bad we can't convey that to Kronkite," said Darla. "That's another project for him."

"There's a lot to be learned from plants," said Evelyn.

Atom grinned. "Okay, sweetheart. I'll bite. What should we learn from plants?" Whenever the subject of plants came up, Evelyn's mind went into high gear.

"I know it amuses you," she said, "nonetheless it's true."

"I believe it," said Orwell. "Would you believe she's now got me talking to the plants? Now when I go into the greenhouse, I feel like a plant cheerleader. GO TEAM GROW!"

They all had a good laugh at Orwell's new found enthusiasm, particularly Evelyn. "There's one variable I haven't been able to tabulate yet in my analysis," she said.

"What's that?" Atom asked.

"Orwell's added contribution of exhaled carbon dioxide," smiled Evelyn.

"Hey, I told you. My hot air is finally good for something."

They all laughed again.

"All right, so we're benefiting plants by breathing, and plants benefit us by providing food and oxygen," said Atom, gesturing first with his right hand, then his left... "It's a good trade, although it doesn't teach us anything except maybe cooperation."

"There's more than that they teach us," said Evelyn.

"For instance...?" Atom liked to tease out his wife's serious side.

"I'll tell you what people should learn from plants. Plants have natural rhythm."

"Oh, I didn't know that. Of course, I've seen them wave. Otherwise, they don't move much. Ordinarily, don't plants just borrow their rhythm from planet rotation or catch a passing breeze?"

"Yes, that's true. Still, they keep time well. In your musical parlance, they can keep the beat. To begin with, people tend to work in fits and starts, no rhythm there— energetic one day, lazy the next— while plants are more reliable. Plants are better workers."

"She's got you there, Atom," laughed Orwell. "Score one for the plant team."

"They grow so slowly, though," said Atom, enjoying the dinner table banter.

"Not really. Look at a corn stalk. Their growth in one season makes us look pretty puny. And what fruit do we bear?"

"She's got you there again," announced Orwell. "More points for the plant team."

"Darla, help," Atom said, kidding some more. "I need better coaching."

Darla laughed. "I'd send you back to the showers, but I'm afraid even Evelyn's plants would fare better in showers than you."

"Okay, I concede. I've been beaten by the plants. I'd better borrow some strategy from their playbook before I compete again," said Atom. "Got any tips for a thrashed opponent?"

"Yes", said Evelyn. "We all would score better if we began to function on a steady basis like plants do. Our output would definitely improve."

"Victory for the plants!" said Atom, raising his arms in surrender.

The mealtime was a whopping success. Everyone left the table filled and happy, and returned with joy to their tasks. Darla and Orwell were spending more time together. They found a game they enjoyed and played it regularly after dinner.

Atom walked to the control room to check Starfarer's autopilot course. With the new charted course, he found their speed had markedly increased after the near collision. Atom wondered if it had anything to do with the wake from the comet. The additional burst of rocket power wasn't sufficient to explain it. The earlier resistance was over. They were now traveling with the aid of some new mysterious force.

He hadn't discussed it with the others because he didn't want to raise their hopes prematurely until he was sure he had found a better course.

He checked his bearings again. He checked his speed. There was a significant difference. Confronted with a barrier before, Starfarer was now getting a boost. Its velocity increased with less drag. He had discovered an invisible current like a jet stream. They had more than made up for the time lost. They were making more speed than he thought possible. Continuing at this rate, they would reach their galactic destination sooner than expected.

After a day had passed, Atom was bubbling over with the news. With some reluctance, he decided to gather them together in the control room. At the risk of being mistaken, he would show them the log and his calculations and have them check the readings and confirm his findings for themselves.

He found Evelyn, of course, in the greenhouse. Together they pulled Orwell and Darla away from their game to hear the news. Atom concealed his excitement as best he could.

When they were all in the control room, Atom showed them his findings.

They checked the instruments and figures. They were correct.

"You know what this means? If we continue at this rate, we'll reach our new galaxy in a little under a year!"

The Starfarer astronauts leaped, and laughed, and hugged. After the long, long voyage through dismal space, they were coming to a new galaxy where they might find a livable planet. A planet where they might have a new beginning, a new home.

"You know what this calls for?" said Atom. "We need some music and some dancing."

CHAPTER XXVIII

After living confined in their cramped spaceship and enduring years of discouragement and tribulation, the Starfarer astronauts were buoyed on a new tide of optimism. Unbelievably, they had done what few thought possible. It was a centuries-old dream of astronomers and adventurers. Kronkite, the great inventor of the Verity Scanner, conceived the project. He would never know whether it succeeded or not. The astronauts had journeyed from their own star system to another galaxy. They were the first to achieve such a feat. As far as they knew, they had become the first interstellar space explorers.

Their journey was far from over, however. They were like shipwrecked sailors afloat in an endless sea, who swim toward a desert island. What dangers lurk there? Is it inhabited? Can they survive there?

It was a giant step for them to get this far. Always the words of the pessimists hung over the project and haunted them. The naysayers who declared it couldn't be done. So far, they had proved them wrong, but the journey was grueling and far from over. New daunting challenges awaited them.

For the moment though, they were elated. Even though it was only one step, it had been a big step. They celebrated by having a party and dancing. Indeed, it was the first party they had celebrated on the whole trip. The break was much deserved.

As their ship approached their new solar system, they gazed at it with renewed hope. They were like visitors assessing a new neighborhood. Within days, the astronauts would reach the outermost planet. The thrill was akin to a tourist traveling to an exotic land. Out of the void, they were nearing a star that was more than just a dot twinkling far in the distance. It was a near star whose brilliance produced sunshine.

Darla increased her activity at the ROSS scanner. She displayed the dogged persistence of a slot machine gambler. After years of deep night flying through emptiness, Atom made more frequent visits to the pilothouse to make observations and discover as much as he could. They were all telescopically excited to see what was before them. Their anticipation would have been greater, if they could have been assured there would be a positive outcome in store for them. The long trip had tested their fortitude.

"Atom!"

Atom jumped, startled as if there was an impending danger.

"Come listen!"

Darla was excitedly waving her hands at the radio console. Atom left his chart-making and walked over to Darla at the ROSS scanner.

"Hear that?" she asked.

Atom could hear a faint sound.

"It's the first I've heard since leaving home, after that disappointing X-ray static. It sounds promising." It was as momentous to her as a footprint in the sand to a stranded sailor on a desert island.

"What do you think it is?"

"I don't know yet, but I'm certainly glad to have something to work with. She reached over and switched on the recorder. "I'll record this now and hope for more tomorrow." She was as excited as a child getting a first birthday card in the mail.

"That's terrific, Darla."

She spoke rapidly. "I just happened on that frequency, and there it was. I can't wait to tell Orwell. I'll have him help me analyze it on the computer. That is, if I can get him away from the greenhouse. That wife of yours is turning him into a regular farmer."

Atom laughed. "She is persuasive, isn't she?"

"I don't mind, just as long as it's only flower beds she gets him into."

It was hard for Darla to fall asleep that night. Her excitement kept Orwell awake. Finally, he convinced her that they should sleep. Before falling to sleep, they made love. Their relationship greatly improved since the Verity Scanner confrontation had cleared the air. They slept cuddled close together most of the night.

Evelyn joined Atom in the pilothouse. He wanted to make some telescopic observations of the galaxy ahead. He wanted to see what planets they might have, and count them. For the first time since their fateful launch, he let his mind entertain the thought of locating a habitable planet. One that they might land on and make their home.

Moving from one geographical location to another— trying to pick a neighborhood, a street, a house— is stressful enough. Here, there were no city guides, no friendly real estate agent to ease the way. There was no guarantee that a habitable planet here even existed. Atom didn't allow his mind to dwell on that awful possibility. The thought was too dreadful. It haunted him anyway.

This new galaxy that they had chosen had characteristics similar to their former one. It had a single star with a rather flat spiral of planets around it. The orbiting planets looked something like a pancake when viewed from the side. After launching into space, they'd been able to look back at their former galaxy and get a good remote view of it. This new planetary system resembled their former one. That gave Atom hope of what he might expect to find in this new one.

Atom had rejected the stars that had deformed or barrel-shaped spirals, and those with large hubs, or those that were globular-shaped. He also ruled out binary star systems. It was too difficult to contemplate what it would be like to live in one of those solar systems, especially those with so much perturbation. The more exotic galaxies appeared to contain too many stars or too much dust and gas.

The closer they approached this solar system, Atom could see it was a much simpler one. In its center, the sun-star was more prominent now. Atom estimated that it was not quite as large as the one they had left, but its strong similarity was reassuring. Indeed, encouraging. The view he saw reminded him a lot of the views he still recalled from back home.

It was a welcomed sight after the years of traversing the void of space. It acted upon his senses like a handrail to a precipice— something to cling to. Space has a dizzying effect on beings oriented to gravity. Maybe that's why someone who is not getting anywhere is said to be drifting.

"There it is," said Atom. "What do you think of it?"

"It's not exactly a cottage in the country yet," said Evelyn, looking at the planetary system. "But, it will have to do. As long as we can find a place to live where plants will grow."

Sitting in the pilothouse, belted in, one could almost imagine Atom and Evelyn as a couple locked in each other's arms, parked in a lover's lane gazing at the stars. When, in fact, they were a part of the whole starry show themselves.

"So far, I've counted eight planets and thirty-four satellites. I keep recounting, because I'm never quite sure whether I've counted one twice, missed one, or found others behind the star."

"Have you made a tentative selection yet?" asked Evelyn. "I'm hoping that the knowledge we bring with us from home will be of value."

"In what way?"

"This is my theory. Please don't just rubber-stamp it to make me feel good. I want you to use all the best thinking you can muster to blow holes in it— the good old scientific way."

"All right, fire away." said Evelyn.

"Think back to our home planet."

"Okay, I'm thinking."

Atom gathered his thoughts. "All the life of our planet was located within an atmospheric layer of about three miles approximately, including your beloved greenery."

"Yes," smiled Evelyn, "that's true. You're not trying to sugarcoat your proposition, thinking I'll let you off easy, are you?"

"No," replied Atom. "I know you better than that. I'm only embellishing for dramatic effect. After all, every presentation should have a little pizzazz."

Evelyn laughed. "Just be careful you don't pizzazz away your credibility."

"I'll be careful," smiled Atom, enjoying Evelyn's comic reply.

"Very well, continue."

"This biosphere, or life zone, is a mere peel around a grapefruit. Compared to matter, and all of space, it is infinitesimal, right?"

"And without plants, it would be infinitely more infinitesimal," joked Evelyn.

"Infinitely so. But seriously, as I see it, the conditions necessary for that fragile rind of life, so to speak, are temperature and the components of air and water."

"Right."

"Think back to the planets we experienced on our journey," said Atom.

"All right, I am."

"Do you remember the first one, not counting our own?"

"Yes."

"What was its condition?"

"Mostly stony."

"That's right. No sign of water or air. The second planet? Do you remember that one?" asked Atom.

"Yes. That one appeared to be all fiery clouds, eruptions, and gases."

"Too hot, wasn't it? And the third and last? The outer most one?"

"That one was too cold," said Evelyn.

"Precisely. This is the point I'm driving at. The planets farther from the star center will probably be too cold for life. Those too close, on the other hand, will probably be too hot. The most likely planet candidates will be those within a certain life-belt range around the star. Just as life on our planet was limited to the troposphere. Does that make sense to you?"

"Yes. That sounds reasonable enough. Water and atmosphere are necessary to support life. Can a planet have an atmosphere without plants? I don't think so. That may be why the first planet was all stone, no atmosphere."

"I can't say for certain but it could have something to do with elements that collected in the birth of that planet. Or it may be determined by gravity, or its rotation rate, whether it can hold an atmosphere."

"That's plausible. How will we know?" asked Evelyn.

"We can check for gases with the spectroscope. If we can trust any of

135

the knowledge we have about our own planet, let's hope the same rules apply all through the cosmos. I figure the planets at a midway point from their star, will be the best candidates for us. At least that's the most reasonable theory I've been able to come up with," said Atom.

"Makes sense to me, sweetheart," Evelyn agreed.

"If only Kronkite and Sara could be here to see this," said Atom, sadly.

They spent another hour charting the galaxy and considering every possibility that came to mind. Then they unstrapped and rode "the can" down and headed off to bed. Looking at the stars as astronauts, rather took the romance out of stargazing.

The Starfarer astronauts had arrived at their new sought for destination. Could it provide them a home? It was a hope cloaked in uncertainty.

CHAPTER XXIX

There is nothing more destructive of happiness than hopelessness. When one is trapped in a stifling situation and unable to extricate oneself, it destroys all sense of pleasure and delight. After the malaise of their years of interstellar voyage through space, the older but wiser astronauts rebounded in energy. The sight of the new solar system, vast as it was, raised their spirits. It affected them like travelers on a long and tiring journey, who begin to read signs announcing arrival at their destination.

Atom had made a chart of the new planets, and he and Orwell were in the control room studying them. They were bent over the chart table with the intensity of two people working on a picture puzzle. Their eyes were fixed on the charts. Atom was pointing with a pen as he described his findings.

"I may be mistaken, but as near as I can calculate with the limited instruments I have, this is the outer planet. The fifth and sixth planets are the largest. I haven't been able to estimate their orbits or rotation yet. They will not be in conjunction so that we can view them all at one time while we fly in."

"Do you think that'll be a problem?" asked Orwell.

"Not if we're lucky. It's my theory based on experience with our own galaxy that the third and fourth planets are in the life-belt zone. I base that on them being not too close or too far from their star." And this line here?"

"That's the trajectory I've plotted. We'll shoot by the outermost planet orbit and pick up a little gravity assist. Then we'll aim for the sixth planet and just bypass it to give us a visual check and use its gravitation to retard our speed. That will bring us into proximity with the third or fourth planet. Since their orbit around the star is much smaller than the outermost planets, we shouldn't have any difficulty observing them. We may even reach them when they're in opposition."

"That sounds good to me," said Orwell. "Real good."

"Think what the astronomers back home would give to see this and have the information that's on this chart, hey? Too bad we can't fax it back to them. Kronkite would be as proud as a new papa."

"I wonder how Kronkite and Sara are doing?" said Atom. "Wonder if he took Sara on that vacation he promised her?"

137

"Vacations were difficult for him, but I'm sure he would have kept his promise. If not, I wouldn't have put it past her to have him hauled before the Verity Scanner," mused Orwell. "That device is capable of righting a lot of wrongs."

"They'd be up in years now. I wonder if they are still alive?"

"Kronkite?" Orwell made a dismissive gesture with his hand. "With all his unfinished projects, he'll never die. I can see him going on forever."

Atom grinned. "Yeah, you're right. Kronkite was indomitable."

Later, Atom and Evelyn were in their room getting ready for bed. A knock on the door surprised them. It was strange because in all their years on Starfarer, it had never happened before. It reminded Atom and Evelyn of their life back home when they'd say: 'Who's there?' or 'We don't need any.'

Atom opened the door.

"Hi." It was Darla and Orwell. "Don't mean to disturb you, but we couldn't wait to tell you. We've just completed a computer analysis of the radio signal Darla picked up on ROSS. It shows every indication of having an intelligent grammar and syntax."

"That's great, Darla!" said Atom. "Isn't that great, sweetheart?"

Evelyn dressed in her nightgown was beaming, too.

"Yeah", said Orwell, "the way they keep repeating the message, it must be a commercial advertising some product."

"We'll keep working on it to see if we can attach some meaning to it; see if it has a vocabulary."

"I hope you don't mind us not waiting till morning to tell you about it," said Darla.

"Not at all. We're glad you did. That's the most promising news yet. Keep at the translation."

"Good night, Evelyn. Good night, Atom," said Orwell and Darla as they hurried back to the computer room to continue their decoding.

Atom closed the door after them.

"Oh, Atom, isn't that marvelous! Our first radio message. I hope it's coming from these planets."

"Wouldn't that be a good sign? I hope it proves to be a deliberately broadcast message and not a natural phenomenon like that X-ray fiasco."

"I hope so, too. Darla spent so much time on that. I felt sorry for her," said Evelyn, climbing back into bed. "She worked so hard on those noise emissions."

Atom and Evelyn— all hope— soon drifted happily back to sleep. Evelyn dreamt she was outdoors in the sunshine with blue sky all around. There were white clouds and bluebirds flying, and flowers, yellow, red and violet blooming all around her in every direction. She just wanted to leap and dance, and sing, and romp. She was so happy.

The next morning, they met Darla and Orwell in the dining room and had their meals together.

Atom noticed that Darla didn't look too well. "How did the decoding go?" He hesitated to ask her about it, then decided there was no point in skirting it.

"It went pretty well," said Orwell. "We have divided the sections into what seem to constitute thought patterns. We're looking for nominatives and predicates, as well as repetitions that would set them apart. It's very much like trying to break a code."

"Don't overdo it, Darla," said Atom. "Are you getting enough sleep?"

"I think so. I just felt a little sick to my stomach this morning. Strange, we haven't made any unusual maneuvers with Starfarer, have we? I thought I'd outgrown the tendency to get motion sickness and adapted well by now to the artificial gravity. Oh well, it'll pass."

"Maybe you're just overly excited about the ROSS signals," said Evelyn.

"I've been thinking, as we've been trying to decipher the radio messages," said Orwell, "what are these inhabitants going to look like? Maybe they'll be green with one eye in the middle of their belly."

"I hope not green," said Evelyn. "I'm used to my plants staying put. I wouldn't like green-looking creatures walking around. I'd always think they would need to be watered, trimmed, and potted, or something."

"What do you think, Atom?" asked Orwell.

"I haven't given it much thought. I've been so intent on just getting to some place livable. I didn't consider who might possibly be there to greet us, or what they might look like. It never crossed my mind. As I think about it now, the most reasonable prospect I can imagine would be landing in a wilderness with lots of wild plants for Evelyn and some not-so-wild animals. Sort of like our ancestors experienced who were explorers. What do you think?" Atom asked.

"The creatures might be horrible with scales and horns and tails," joked Orwell, playfully. "They might be cannibalistic and breathe fire. They could hide in holes waiting to pounce on unwary travelers and drag them kicking and screaming into their underground caves."

"Well, whatever. I hope the plants, at least, are more friendly that that," said Evelyn. "If not, I'm not going to like the place."

"I wasn't feeling too well *before*," said Darla. "Now I'm feeling worse. I think I'll go to bed early tonight."

"Sorry, honey. I was just joking, I hope I didn't upset you," said Orwell apologetically.

"I think you've watched too many horror movies, Orwell. Besides, whatever these inhabitants look like, they must be intelligent or how could they be sending out messages?" said Atom.

"That's right, they must be intelligent monsters, or crafty. I don't know which...." Suddenly, the radar siren went off with its loud shrill screech!

Atom and Orwell dashed out of the dining room and up the hallway. Evelyn and Darla followed.

"Should we head for the control or the pilothouse?" asked Orwell.

"Evelyn, you and Darla check the control room. Orwell and I will ride "the can" up to the pilothouse and make a visual check. Brace yourselves for a diversionary move in case it turns out to be another comet."

Evelyn made it to the control room first and looked at the surveillance screen. An object was coming toward them.

Shortly after, Atom and Orwell had ridden up to the pilothouse, they stared out the window.

"What the heck? It's a small object. It has a rather irregular shape. Not at all like an asteroid," said Orwell. "It looks like something manufactured."

"A two-degree correction should make it pass us by safely," said Atom. "One left throttle burst."

Orwell hit the lever and Starfarer veered to the left of the flying object.

"In all our travels, that has to be the strangest space material I've seen so far," said Orwell. "Look, it appears to be constructed of some metal cone with antennae on it."

It was an amazing sight for all the astronauts to witness. They had not seen anything like it in all their years of space travel.

After Starfarer had met the object and passed it, Atom and Orwell looked at each other thunderstruck. Their mouths gaped and their eyes were disbelieving.

"That was no random conglomeration of space material. That was an intelligently manufactured object," said Atom.

"I don't doubt it, but what was it? If it was a spacecraft, the creatures aboard would have to be pretty small, maybe the size of insects or elves. It seemed to be a conical-shaped device with rods, evidently nothing living on it," said Orwell, sitting back in his seat.

"Whatever it was, where could it have come from? Not from back home, that's for sure. Therefore, it's the first sign we're not alone in this solar system!" said Atom.

For the rest of the time the astronauts spent together before Atom and Evelyn went to bed, they discussed the implications of the strange object. It served to take Darla's mind off her earlier queasy feeling. Like a sailor who spots a land bird, this was another hopeful sign of other intelligent life. It inspired Darla and Orwell to greater effort in decoding the radio receptions.

All of them made more frequent trips to the pilothouse to gaze telescopically out. Perhaps hoping to spot some other similarly fabricated objects. No more were seen.

That night, when Orwell and Darla went to bed, Orwell had a dream. It turned into more of a nightmare. He had allowed his mind to imagine too many gruesome creatures ahead on a planetary welcoming committee. Some perhaps inspired by horror movies he had watched. In his dream, he saw devils with pointed ears, scales, and tails, grimacing fangs and fiery eyes.

As often happens with those who fashion such demons out of bad meals, or bad motives, he suffered that night by twisting and turning restlessly. It never pays to concoct monsters, for they really will exist in the minds of their creators.

The next day, the astronauts expected to have a close-up of the first planet, since leaving their own, that might be habitable— one they could call… 'home'.

CHAPTER XXX

The now elderly Kronkite, inventor of the Verity Scanner and organizer of the Starfarer Space Project, sat at his kitchen table enjoying a leisurely breakfast with his wife.

Sara looked wistfully at her husband while she refilled his coffee cup. "Don't you wonder what became of our Starfarer astronauts?"

"Yes, all the time. They were fine young people," he reflected. "Atom, Evelyn, Darla, and Orwell. They were like family, weren't they? I'll never forget the day they entered the gantry and waved goodbye. The look on their faces."

"Do you think they found a habitable planet?"

"We'll never know, will we?" said Kronkite. "We'll never know."

                    *   *   *

Meanwhile, light-years away speeding through the vast immensity of an unknown and uncharted space, the Starfarer astronauts flew on. Their nebular cosmic scenery looked like a painter's splatter technique; luminous dots on a dark background. Some of the splotches were spirals, some resembled fuzzy oranges, some were shaped like spinning pizzas, others like swirling clouds. Approaching in Starfarer, the astronauts observed the orbiting planets, their view sometimes lost in the glare of the star. Held in tow by the star's powerful gravitational pull, the planets circled in a flattened elliptical disc pattern around the star's massive center.

They gazed in awe at the wondrous sight.

"I don't know how you managed it, but you did it, old boy. I must admit there were times I had given up traversing that huge void," Orwell exclaimed. "But you did it. You brought us through."

Evelyn and Darla were all smiles.

After years of traveling through the monotonous night, avoiding dust clouds, asteroids, and comets, the astronauts looked forward with eager anticipation at the celestial bodies before them. Would one of the planets of this solar system turn out to be a new home for them?

The Starfarer astronauts, wearing special lenses, sat in their pilothouse seats to view the spectacle. Whereas, on leaving their own galaxy, they

142

had pointed away from their star. Now, they directly faced one. Their specially designed glasses permitted them to look at the planetary system. A portion of the lenses blocked out the star glare entirely while the rest of the lens protected them from damaging rays. The only way to distinguish the galactic matter from other stars billions of light-years away, was the orbiting motion of the planets and the fact that they stood out by the reflected light from the star. The near ones were about like quarter moons and the far ones were like illuminated polka dots.

Having endured much of their adult life traveling in space, the astronauts had no illusions about it. They had none of the cockiness of some inexperienced land-bound ignoramuses. No fanciful bombastic claims of human supremacy over the cosmos. They dealt with physical reality every day and didn't indulge in that kind of absurd thinking.

Perhaps the smaller mind of the person, the larger the need for such grandiose delusions.

Explorers that they were, they saw things in proper perspective. They were only one small part of the cosmos, not the center of it.

After living in an artificial environment for so many years, the astronauts knew their vulnerability and adapted to it. There hope was to find a new planet to live on that would have a natural environment. How big a long-shot was that? On that chance, they had staked everything. What was there in the human psyche that explores and keeps on advancing, no matter what the risk?

It had been years since Atom first flew close to a planet. As they approached now, he hoped he hadn't lost his touch. Doubly dangerous was the fact that each planet had its own idiosyncrasies. At Starfarer's velocity, everything happened quickly. Not much room to correct any errors.

Besides, he had never landed a spaceship like Starfarer. No one ever had. It preyed on his mind.

The astronauts watched as they approached the outermost planet. It was an odd color and reflected a lot of light. They had checked it with their instruments and suspected it would be very cold.

"I'm not sure. It might have a methane atmosphere," said Atom. "Not a good planet for gardening, sweetheart. Not for your varieties, anyway. Probably the seasons would be all wrong, too. How long this planet would take to make an orbit, I don't know."

"Gee, if it's slow, it would be hard waiting for summer," quipped Orwell, hoping to relieve some of the tension with humor.

"Yeah," said Atom. "It'd probably make our winters back home seem like the tropics."

"This is definitely not the source of our radio signals," said Darla. "Any radio operator there would have to dress in his woolies."

"Or freeze his asteroid off," laughed Orwell. "I'd like a planet with a good summer season for baseball. Matter of fact, I'd like to be a team owner."

"Oh, baby," said Darla, "you did love your sports, didn't you?"

"Yeah," sighed Orwell. "The king of swat, couldn't hit a homer like I could out here in space. That baseball would go on forever unless it was caught by a black hole."

"Oh look, there's one of the planet's moons," said Darla. "Moons have lost a lot of their glamour since I've seen them up close."

"Hope you don't lose any of your passion as a result," said Orwell. "I've always counted on a moon as an ally."

"Maybe another moon will be conducive," said Atom. "I think this planet might have more than one. I've lost count." Atom had lost interest in recording such information without Kronkite to report to with such facts. Everything now was in support of Starfarer's navigation.

The nervous levity gave way to more serious concentration as Starfarer entered the range of the planet's gravity. Atom and Orwell were ready at the controls. They then felt the planet's gravitational pull slingshot them forward. They were on the way to the innermost planets. These were in the area that Atom had designated as the "life-belt" region, the ones that held the most promise for habitation.

"I felt a little rusty at the controls," admitted Atom. "But that assist went off all right. You okay, Darla?"

"This morning I felt a little queasy, just apprehensive, I think. I held my cookies okay with that maneuver. Now that we're shooting away from that big planet, I'll see if our radio signals improve any. You want to join me Evelyn? Maybe they speak your language."

"Yes, I'll join you after I check the greenhouse. Sometimes the acceleration shakes up my plants."

Darla and Evelyn rode "the can" down. The novelty of being weightless had long ago worn off. They moved about using favorite handholds so familiarly they never gave it a second thought.

Orwell grew thoughtfully quiet. "You know," he said, after the wives had left, "whenever we're together in here, I can't help remembering the time I attacked you. Now, when I think about it, I feel terrible."

"Forget it. I forgave you for that a long, long time ago," said Atom. He gave Orwell a pat on the shoulder. "It takes a real man to apologize, in my book. And you're a real man. Come on, let's go down and get a snack. I set Starfarer on autopilot."

They reached the galley and prepared themselves a little snack. Usually lighthearted and playful, Orwell this time was in a serious frame of mind.

"Do you ever think about where we're heading?" he asked.

Atom was surprised by Orwell's earnestness. Orwell had matured so much from the young man he remembered years back on launch day.

"Yes, I think about where we're going all the time. I take my reckoning, I chart a course, and try to get there. Of course, when you're going somewhere nobody's been before, it's not easy. Not like having a map and knowing your destination. Is that what you mean?"

"No, I was thinking in a larger sense," said Orwell.

"You mean like living and dying?"

Both men became quite subdued by the solemnness of the discussion.

"No, not exactly. I know death is a reality. I can accept that."

"That's more than most people can do," said Atom.

"I'm thinking more about where we're heading in life."

"Well, let's turn it around," said Atom. "Let me ask you, what's your idea on it?"

"You know, I don't know what to think. Does anybody really give it much thought?" Orwell ate his snack without actually tasting it. "I guess everybody thinks about it once in a while. Don't they?"

"Most the time, I'm too busy." Atom watched Orwell work the thought over in his mind.

"After liftoff and the excitement was over, I started to get angry about being here. I was full of regret, and I sure took it out on everybody. I'm sorry about it now."

Orwell stopped to reflect before continuing, "I was wishing I was back home, and all those recruits who weren't chosen, wished they were in my shoes. Strange, isn't it? It seems like no matter what you choose, no one is ever satisfied."

Atom smiling, nodded. "I know what you mean."

"It doesn't make a whole lot of sense, does it? For a brief moment you're content, and then you're restless again."

"And, heading on...." said Atom.

"That's it. Heading on." They clicked glasses and laughed.

"I think I know one thing for sure," said Orwell. "It doesn't pay to take oneself too seriously, does it? It just *is*. So, take it as it comes."

Atom had to laugh. "I don't know why, but that makes a lot of sense."

Atom and Orwell were having a hearty laugh when Evelyn and Darla rushed in. The look on their faces and the way they stood indicated they had something important to report.

"We've got some news for you!"

"Oh?" said Orwell. "Did you crack the radio code messages?"

"No, not yet," said Darla.

"What is it then?"

"I'm pregnant!"

CHAPTER XXXI

The announcement of Darla's pregnancy came as a surprise to them all. Suddenly, the whole Starfarer mission had a new sense of purpose. Also, it imposed a sense of urgency on Atom to find a habitable planet. Toward this end, he used every means to accelerate the journey.

"I thought they were taking precautions like us," said Atom to Evelyn, as she harvested and gathered some vegetables from the greenhouse to take up to the galley.

"They were. It's just one of those things you can't avoid sometimes." Evelyn finished putting some of her veggies into her basket.

"Well, it's both exciting and frightening at the same time. We hadn't considered raising families on Starfarer," said Atom, reflecting on it.

"The four of us have managed so far. I guess we can provide for a little one," said Evelyn.

"That part's all right. What if we don't find a habitable planet? Is it fair to the child?"

"You'll just have to keep your Kronkite optimism working, sweetheart," she said, picking up her basket.

Starfarer had gained speed at the eighth planet. Atom hadn't discovered the ninth, which was truly the outermost. Because its orbit was behind the star, the spaceship picked up an additional gravity assist from the seventh planet and bypassed another making a distant orbit. The sixth planet was one of the most resplendent exotic-looking ones they had ever seen on their long journey. The four astronauts spent several hours in the pilothouse marveling at it.

Atom had calculated that it was the second largest of the group. It was very brilliant— almost like a bright sun in reflected colorful light. It had a thick atmosphere, possibly of methane and ammonia, and was apparently extremely cold. Luminescent rings were its most impressive feature. It affected the astronauts like a natural scenic wonder affects a land-bound traveler. After years of dark space, it was an attractive change of scenery.

Within three months, Starfarer arrived at the fifth and largest planet. The nearer they came to the central star hub, the more closely were the planets ringed. The fifth planet was huge. So far as they could surmise, it was also unfit for life, having a dense atmosphere. Large swirling reddish-orange spots rotated over its surface. It appeared to have a very fast rotation. Atom counted at least a dozen moons.

Atom was becoming excited and nervous. They were nearing the region he had designated as the "life-belt". This was the area, he reasoned, that would most likely be fit for habitation. So much of what he had striven for was hanging in the balance. He didn't dare think of the consequences, if they were forced to seek another star. It was just too disheartening. Sometimes his jaw became very tight when he thought of all that was at stake.

Every day, Darla spent hours at the ROSS scanner and in the computer room with Orwell trying to decipher the signals she received. Even with the aid of the computer, the task was proving to be difficult. Realistically, she knew it might take years to accomplish. She approached the task as if within the next minute, she might make a breakthrough.

All of a sudden, the radar siren sounded its warning screech. They dropped their decoding and raced to the control room. Orwell met Atom in the hallway. They sped to "the can", rode up, and quickly buckled-up into their seats.

All through space, they had endured months of boredom. Within the galaxy, they would have to be on high alert, especially with so much loose debris circling the star, and Starfarer traveling at a high rate of speed.

There were blips of light crossing the radar screen.

"What is it?" asked Orwell catching his breath. Then he looked out the window and saw a curving band of stony bits. It resembled a rainbow made of rocks.

"It's an asteroid belt," said Atom. "We'll be safe if we don't tangle with it. It didn't show up well until it was right upon us. We'll have to take some evasive action. Hope the gals are buckling up. Better call down to alert them. Stand by the throttles."

The stony ring was an awesome sight.

In the spaceship, they were on the blind side of the belt. It took the star glare to light it. Debris like bullets, flew past out of the dazzling backdrop.

"Our only hope is to climb out of this plane and hope no stragglers nail us. Full on the right rocket! We'll go with the flow, then hope to climb out of it."

Starfarer responded.

"Hope the gals got your call, Orwell."

A voice came over the intercom. It was Evelyn. "Don't worry about us. We're in our restraints."

Aware of the radar warning, Darla and Evelyn had hastened to the control room, and, as seasoned space travelers, buckled up.

A hail of dust beat against Starfarer's hull like pelting rain. The spaceship climbed free and clear.

Atom was about to heave a sigh of relief, when it happened. They felt a jarring blow. It hit aft, driving the spaceship into a dizzying spin. Atom stayed at the controls, but like a car on ice, it was not responding. It was all the astronauts could do not to blackout.

Atom cursed silently. Had they come this far only to crash into oblivion?

A seeming eternity of gyrations followed. The stabilizer was struggling to cope with the assault. Seconds stood between recovery or annihilation. If control could not be regained, Starfarer would go on plummeting through space wherever their spinning trajectory pointed them. The four astronauts would be helplessly pinned to their seats with no possibility of moving about or making repairs.

"Regardless of what's ahead, give it all we've got, Orwell. It's our only chance to right ourselves."

If the damage to the rear rocket was severe, Atom knew the engine might blow. They themselves might end up just another exploding bit of matter in space.

The strain on the astronauts was intense. It was a moment of truth. What an expression, thought Atom. If only truth could survive such calamities, and falsehood be obliterated, how much better the universe would be. But falsehood would always exist. And so would calamity. Truth and peace would always require effort to survive.

They felt the jolt of the rocket blast. Starfarer wobbled and tried to regain its course. Atom feathered the controls. He and the spaceship became inseparable partners in the battle for survival.

Orwell nervously found a moment to interject some fatalistic levity. "Yow, what a greeting that was. They must not like us here. Throwing rocks at us like that."

It was a good and healing remark.

"If this is it," said Atom, "we may as well go out with a smile as any other way. Only the slow-witted think intelligent is being somber."

They enjoyed a moment of humor. It dispelled some of the tension.

Slowly, ever so gently, the equilibrium of the spaceship was recovered. Then, with painstaking care, Atom checked and righted their bearings. Their path was clear. He could reset their former course and the autopilot.

"When you said we'd have to climb out of this plane," chuckled Orwell, "I didn't think of the asteroid plane at first. It sounded to me like you were saying we'd have to abandon ship. Words sure can get slippery when you try to grasp their meaning."

"I see what you mean," smiled Atom. "I'll try to be more explicit next time."

"Don't bother, said Orwell. "I don't want another time like the one we just had."

They both laughed.

The next two days were spent assessing the damage. The integrity of their living quarters was maintained. Their artificial gravity still functioned. They had taken a hit on one of the rear rockets. It was damaged, but not totally disabled. They survived the battering, but their propulsion for interstellar travel was compromised.

Atom knew what that meant. Future options were now severely limited. The offshoot of the asteroid bombardment, bound them to this star system forever. Of the four planets ahead, it was absolutely imperative that one of them be suitable and habitable for life.

CHAPTER XXXII

"Any progress?" asked Atom. He had just come from the pilothouse after making some instrument checks and observing their next planet. He knew that Orwell and Darla were working on recorded radio signals from the ROSS scanner in the computer room.

Orwell frowned and Darla didn't look any happier.

"We've isolated these various sounds— more than forty of them— and found frequent repetitions. Some of them can easily be used in phrases and sentences. The problem is, to what do the sounds refer? Not unexpectedly, our language has no correlation to this one," said Darla, rubbing the back of her neck which ached from trying to transcribe the phonemes into words with meaning.

"It just sounds like gobbledygook to me," said Orwell.

"I really think there is a language here if we could find the key," said Darla.

To Atom, it was a thread of hope, an important thread. He hoped Darla was right. It was the only hope they had that any of the four remaining planets ahead would support life.

"How does the next planet look?" Orwell asked, exhausted from the listening and decoding effort and wanting to take a break.

"It appears to have a good rotation. Goes around about once every twenty-four hours or so. The temperature looks somewhat favorable, too. It's in the "life-belt" zone. Very similar to our home planet's distance to its sun-star."

The mere mention of 'home planet' brought visions of the home they had left behind. Time and absence had turned their former planet into a paradise of memories— trees, valleys, rivers, and mountains. Everything made beautiful by nostalgia.

"When will we get a view of the next planet?" asked Darla.

"Yeah," said Orwell, "I want to be awake to see it."

"Don't worry, I'll let you know when," said Atom. "By the way, Darla, how do you feel today? Any better?"

"All right. I was sick to my stomach a lot as a kid, so I think I've had good preparation for space travel and motherhood."

Atom laughed. "Well, I'm going to the greenhouse to see Evelyn. See you later. Keep up the good work."

True to his word, when the time came, Atom had them all gather in the pilothouse to view their first likely candidate for a home. Like their former planet, it was a terrestrial one. The distance from the source of light and heat could be favorable for life.

"I haven't spotted any romantic moons yet, Orwell. I just thought I'd give you fair warning."

"Ha," said Orwell. "I guess I could handle that."

"He could," Darla agreed.

"Evelyn will just have to be content to grow sunflowers, and no moon flowers." joked Orwell.

The distance between Starfarer and the planet quickly closed. As it did, their hopes turned to disappointment. It was better than any planet they had so far visited, but it was nothing like home. The instruments didn't indicate any atmosphere. No lush vegetation. There might be some moss or lichens. That was all. Hardly a promising homeland for space colonists.

"The place could benefit from some intensive farming," said Evelyn. "If there was a way to find water."

"What good would that do? I don't have any recipes for moss and lichens," quipped Orwell.

Orwell's attempt at humor was lost in their shattered hopes.

Atom felt leaden. His "life-belt" theory was only partially vindicated. He was beginning to feel inadequate as a leader; a lost scout who couldn't find his way. It was a helpless feeling. It was frustrating. It was like he was letting Kronkite down, but mostly failing Evelyn and Darla and Orwell.

Atom went to bed that night with a troubled mind. Evelyn sensed his brooding and comforted him. It helped him to find peace and finally sleep.

The next morning, Orwell let Darla work on the decoding herself. He decided to experiment with video reception. He thought if someone, some place, was broadcasting radio, why not television. Besides, he was tired of trying to assign meaning to radio sounds.

Atom prepared his navigation for the next planet. He began to feel dulled by his failures. Efforts do not build happily on failure. He felt his choices, like the confines of Starfarer, were becoming narrower day by day. Was he the cause of the asteroid damage because of some errors he had made?

He tried to remember the counsels of his mentor, Kronkite, who he tried to exemplify. What would he have advised? Never brood about what's past, only think about the future. It's the only way to get things done. Have patience, perseverance, optimism. Good words that, to Atom, now sounded so very hollow. The others had trusted his navigation, and he felt he had let them down.

Atom made his calculation mechanically. At their current speed, they would soon intercept the orbit of the next planet. Darla's ROSS signals still offered them some hope.

On the first day, nothing happened. Atom tried to conceal his impatience. As his apprehension grew, he fidgeted with his charting instruments. Had he missed something?

The following day was similar to the one before. Sometimes Atom wished Evelyn wasn't always so preoccupied with the greenhouse. He was in need of encouragement. Ridiculous. What could she say or do? Besides, he knew how important her work was. He knew what their situation was. No words could change or fix that. They must find a new planet home or live out their lives forever on Starfarer.

Darla kept at her ROSS console. There were more signals than ever. Orwell worked with the television. One day he thought he had a ghost of an image on his screen. He became very excited, but ended up suspecting his own imagination had played a trick on him. Each in his own way filled time with activities that suppressed their sense of hopelessness.

Eight more days passed. They had reached the halfway point. They were eager to see the next planet. All the while, anxiety grew with their anticipation. They ate quietly in the dining room.

"Today," said Evelyn, "is the anniversary of our launch day." Evelyn kept track of special days. It fit in with her attention to planting days.

"I feel older, but not wiser," said Orwell. "Sara would never have gotten her vacation had she come with us. Maybe that's why Kronkite wanted to join us. He could skip vacations. He wasn't much for vacations."

A thought came to Atom which he didn't utter. It was about a lost explorer who left a diary before he perished. It was a morbid thought that he tried to put out of his mind.

"Well," said Atom excusing himself, "I'd better get back to my navigating. Starfarer flies on autopilot, but it needs guidance." He tried to put on a cheerful face for the sake of the others. It would be a face that wouldn't fool the Verity Scanner.

A day later, Darla had more radio signals than she could cope with. They added hope but no knowledge. She was convinced they were voices. Rather than help, the multiplicity of phonemes only confused her. Each one seemed to be so different from each other, like a jumble of languages. It was difficult to sort them out. However, it raised her hope that out there was intelligent life. Somewhere.

"Careful, Darla," advised Orwell jokingly, "you'll get irritable *vowel* sickness." He laughed.

Her ROSS efforts did give Orwell further incentive to pursue his video reception idea. He spent his entire day at it, only quitting after he was too bleary-eyed to continue.

Finally, the day arrived. They met together in the pilothouse and buckled into their seats. Light from the sun-star beamed in through the window. It was good to have the sunshine after so many years spent in artificial lighting. It added warmth and cheer. "There it is," said Atom. "Sorry Orwell. I think it only has one moon."

"No problem. In my younger days, I was always too busy to look at the moon anyway."

"What a pretty azure blue," said Darla. "This is prettier than the planet with rings."

"I hope the color is the sign of water," said Atom. "Do those look like polar caps to you?"

At first, it appeared the size of a pea, then it grew to the size of a marble as they approached.

We'll be making a wide circle," said Atom. "We don't want to risk atmospheric friction which would destroy us at this velocity. It'll give us plenty of time for observation."

They were all using telescopes and binoculars.

"Green!" exclaimed Evelyn excitedly. "Green and blue and patches that appear to be continental masses, and all under swirling clouds over the surface. I never thought I would see as beautiful a sight again in my lifetime, as I'm seeing now."

"And that green... what could it be... could it be chlorophyll?" said Evelyn with a grin as wide as her face.

"It's beautiful," marveled Darla.

"It almost makes me feel like I'm home again," said Orwell.

Atom looked at the others and shared their joy. His heart raced. He felt a huge weight drop away from inside. Atom hoped with the others that it wasn't too good to be true. Was it finally to be the culmination and reward for all they had sacrificed and suffered?

"Give me some retrorocket, Orwell," Atom ordered. "We'll establish a wide orbit around this planet and eventually retard our speed and synchronize with the moon's orbit, if we can. In my scope, the moon appears to have craters, and no atmosphere. Clouds on the planet give every indication that it does have an atmosphere. We'll have to approach it very carefully, or we'll burn up like a meteor."

"That's right," said Orwell. "We don't want to go out in a blaze of glory after coming this far."

"Oh, look. What is that?"

They all looked where Darla was pointing. It was a small object, seemingly not like space junk or an asteroid.

"I think it might be some kind of satellite

dish. I'll aim our antenna at it. There, it's pulling a signal right now. I'll put it on our screen."

They all watched with great excitement. They watched like they used to back home, like a family watches a favorite program. All that appeared was a scrambled image of dots and colored squiggles.

"There's something there, all right," said Orwell. "Our reception settings are not matching its transmission. I'll have to work on it."

As they orbited lazily, like a moon around the planet, they spent hours longingly peeking at the distant tiny globe. The sight of it made them shiver and shake for joy. After enduring years of gloomy space travel, had they found a planet home for themselves? Was their long tedious journey at an end? Each had his own private reverie about it. Darla remembered her pleasure shopping. Evelyn imagined gardens and lush landscapes. Orwell dreamed of sports and cheering fans. To Atom, as an orphan, he envisioned a home for Evelyn and himself. Would this be the fulfillment of all their dreams?

CHAPTER XXXIII

The next week was a busy one on Starfarer. The sight of the azure blue planet clothed in a swirl of white clouds gave the four astronauts new purpose and energy. Atom took readings and fitted the telescopic lens to one surveillance camera. Evelyn spent less time in the greenhouse and more time looking for green patches on the multicolored continents. Darla continued deciphering radio signals and trying to pinpoint their location on the globe. Orwell worked to unscramble the video signals. Everyone was totally occupied, elated, and encouraged.

"It is certainly wonderful to see a planet with an atmosphere, after passing all those airless turbulent ones," said Atom. He had just finished making a spectroscopic analysis.

"I've had a thought on that," said Evelyn. "If it has sufficient carbon dioxide to grow plants, I think it could be made a decent place to live. That's my dream."

"Orwell's dream is more occupational. And it's not farming. He'd like to be a real estate agent or own a television station. He's really working hard to see what television channels are being transmitted from that planet," said Darla. "He's a born entrepreneur."

"Or, if we start a colony, I would want to own a bank," said Orwell. "Bankers always did well back home. I can dream, can't I?"

Evelyn laughed, then turned to Atom. "Are you getting good readings from your spectroscopic examinations of the planet?"

"Yes, near as I can figure the planet has about 21% oxygen, 78% nitrogen, and three parts to 10,000 of carbon dioxide."

"That's close to home readings. That is encouraging," said Evelyn. "With enough water and moderate temperature, I can make plants flourish there."

At a great distance, Starfarer circled the planet orbiting behind the moon and revolving about their new sun-star. While the planet was in its dark phase, the astronauts thought they could see areas of illumination on its surface.

"There has to be advanced life on the planet to explain those lighted areas when the planet is not receiving the sun's rays," said Atom.

"Unless we're imagining it," said Orwell. "You know how easily we can be fooled by illusions. It's the worst way of acquiring knowledge. One is more apt to be misinformed than enlightened. Back home, remember the chaos caused by those lying manipulating fakers, before Kronkite invented the Verity Scanner? After that, any belief, unsupported by verifiable proof, couldn't fool people."

The next day, Orwell called everyone into the recreation room. He was the most excited anyone had seen him since the day of the launching.

"Look," he said. "Look closely." He pointed at the television screen. "There are people! People on the planet! And they look like us!"

They were stunned. They looked at the television in disbelief. The people were clothed differently, had different hair styles, but otherwise they looked much like themselves."

"You're having fun with us," said Atom. "You're playing a video disc from one of your sci-fi movies, aren't you?"

"No!" protested Orwell. "I'm picking up that TV signal right off their satellites."

The three sat down amazed and stared at the screen. It was almost beyond belief. They couldn't understand the language spoken, but they recognized humans similar to themselves.

"This is absolutely incredible," said Atom. "Pinch me and tell me I'm not dreaming." It was real. And the others saw it as well. Never had a television show been so captivating as this one was to the weary space travelers. It mattered not at all that they couldn't understand the language. They were completely captivated by what they saw.

"Seems like we're not the first colonists to visit this planet," observed Orwell, grinning broadly, still in disbelief.

"That could be so." said Atom. "We have a lot of studying to do." The news was so startling, that, as jubilant as he was, he felt exhausted by the sheer excitement of it.

Several hours later, the astronauts were still looking at the TV screen. They studied the faces. They counted the fingers. They noted the eyes, ears, and noses. To find people who so resembled themselves light-years away from their former planet was so unexpected, it made them speechless.

They watched the television way past their meals and bedtimes. For so long, they had been alone in space on their journey. They were like explorers who suddenly had discovered a populated city in a wilderness. It was absolutely breathtaking.

During the next seven days, their new planet was the subject of intense study. With the telescopic lens in place, the astronauts took turns observing the planet's surface as it rotated. Atom pursued his study with the meticulousness that would have made Kronkite proud. Orwell was totally absorbed in the planet's TV programs. Darla was making a valiant effort to understand the languages of the inhabitants, at least to acquire some of their vocabulary. "Oh, if I only could figure out what they are saying?"

Evelyn, for once, hurried her greenhouse duties so she might study the flora of the planet. It was a busy time for all. It was a time of purpose-filled concentration.

At mealtimes, they would share discoveries and joyfully compare notes.

"The inhabitants have many forms of transportation, unusual, but recognizable," said Atom. "They appear to have an active maritime. Most of their population centers are located by rivers and seaports."

"I am particularly impressed with their agriculture," Evelyn noted. "There appears to be good arable land and considerable forest area. Some erosion I'm not able to explain. Could be from misuse or climate."

"It appears the planet will offer you opportunities to continue your horticulture, sweetheart," said Atom.

Evelyn smiled. The thought was a satisfying one.

"What do you think of their homes, Evelyn?" asked Darla.

"Much of their housing appears ill-planned, at least that's my impression. Did you notice that? It's almost as if it was treated with secondary importance."

"Some of the TV housing views are attractive. They may only be stage sets, though." Darla conjectured.

"I've watched their sports," said Orwell, "and been appalled by all the barbarism. I don't understand their games fully, but they seem to rely less on skill, speed, and agility, and more on infliction of injury and despicable behavior. In one sport, a player would strike a player in the face with a curved stick. In another, a player would gouge an opponent in the eye, and kick and stomp on him. In another, heavily padded players sought to injure each other, often in covert sneaky ways. Many are carried off the playing fields, injured."

"Yes, I saw some of what you describe," said Darla. She winced at the thought of it. "I couldn't understand the crowd's approval and delight at such cruelty."

"Yes, they seem to take a blood-thirsty glee in it," said Orwell.

"Is the crowd venting a lot of pent-up hostility, do you think?" suggested Evelyn.

"Why would they have so much anger? That's what I wonder about," said Darla, "why so much anger?"

"I wonder about that, too, Darla," said Evelyn. "There seems to be a whole lot of antagonism on the entire planet. I've noticed many armed fortification, artillery, and battle lines. When I viewed a particular section, I was surprised by the craters. I thought the atmosphere protected the planet from such meteor damage. On closer inspection, I discovered it was caused by some form of warfare."

"I'm not surprised," said Orwell.

"You're not?" asked Atom. "Why not?"

"I've watched some of their action-type shows. I didn't have to know the language to follow the plot. Any child could do it. They depend heavily on weapons. There's never any use of reason, mediation, or compassion. Typically, the main character is quite full of himself, very self-righteous, who, when he can't have his own way, uses a weapon to murder one or more opponents. Opponents are always demonized. Murder is one of their idealized behaviors. Every story seems to feature weapons to solve problems."

"It reminds me of the strife our planet used to have," said Atom, "before the invention of the Verity Scanner."

The astronauts ate awhile in silence. What they had seen had affected the joy they at first felt when seeing the beautiful planet.

"Even shows for children are full of violence. Murder is displayed in comic ways," said Orwell.

"Maybe the influence of the shows could encourage the violence?" said Darla.

"I don't think so," said Atom. "I think it's only a symptom. The antagonism must come from somewhere else. But where? You're probably going to say 'why can't people be as peaceable as plants' - aren't you, Evelyn?"

"No," said Evelyn. "It's true. Plants aren't violent, but they do compete for living space."

"With all the space we've seen, there should be enough for us," smirked Orwell. "Especially considering the little space we've become accustomed to."

The astronauts finished their meal and returned to their tasks. Many aspects of the new planet were troubling. Many puzzling. They had come a long way carrying Utopian ideas of what they might find. They had thought maybe to find a wilderness and live in harmony with it. They were pleased to find people like themselves. All the same, they were distressed by the discord they had witnessed.

Despite the unpleasant revelations, they remained optimistic. They were captivated by the beauty and potential of the planet. They hoped they had at last found a new home for themselves. They continued their observations orbiting from afar, eager to learn more about what the planet had to offer. After their long voyage in the cosmos, they had found their first and their only oasis.

CHAPTER XXXIV

Starfarer continued its slow wide orbit around the newly discovered planet. In all their lengthy travel, it was the only celestial body that had an atmosphere, the special living environment they required. With their remote viewing from television reception off TV satellites, which Orwell had set up, the astronauts were in a learning fervor. They wanted to be well-prepared for what was to come. As far as they knew, their presence hadn't been discovered yet. The astronauts were determined to know as much as possible about the new planet before attempting to land there.

Starfarer was equipped with landing gear, but it was all untested. Nobody had ever landed a spaceship exactly like theirs. A lot of preparation would be necessary. Atom had spent hours learning the procedures for landing in flight simulation. but that was many years ago. He was spending a lot of his time now studying the flight manuals to refresh his memory.

One detail stuck in Atom's mind in particular. After they suited up and were strapped into their pilothouse seats, the artificial gravity would have to be stopped. They could not land while their living quarters were revolving. It was somewhat like the launch in reverse. In descent, the artificial gravity of their living quarters would have to end with no known way to restore it.

Selecting a suitable landing place was the next prerequisite. Landing their spaceship weighed heavily on Atom's mind. He studied the flight manuals assiduously hoping to anticipate any contingencies that he might encounter.

There were other concerns as well which troubled Atom and the others as well.

Of course, they all were delighted to discover that they resembled the planet's human inhabitants. However, they themselves were still aliens. Would they be accepted? All in all, there were many unanswered and unanswerable questions.

At the ROSS console, Darla continued to study the planet's languages. She also heard much of what she interpreted to be music broadcast from the planet. Some was melodious, some not. Some sounded more like twanging and yowling, very boring and repetitive.

Evelyn was delighted with the prospects for agriculture feeling that the planet might have good arable land for plants. Orwell was awed by the technological potential that he observed.

Atom was at least relieved that he had found a habitable home for them at last, after traveling so long in barren space. Could he land safely now was his main concern.

"Hi, Atom." It was Darla. She had just ridden "the can" up to the pilothouse. Atom was deep in concentration on the surveillance eyepiece. He looked like a biologist searching for microbes.

"How's the deciphering going, Darla?" he asked.

"I haven't become fluent in any of their languages," she said. "They have so many, even they can't understand each other. So how is an outsider supposed to cope with it? You'd think they would make more of an effort to have a universal language. Maybe that would explain all their discord—lack of communication."

"No doubt that would contribute to strife. It's difficult enough to avoid conflict within a common language." Darla and Atom heard the tubular elevator coming up. Orwell floated in while Darla was buckling into her seat.

"You'll have to let out your belt some, honey," said Orwell patting his wife lovingly on the tummy as he buckled up next to her. Since Darla began to show, Orwell had become extra attentive. There was new domesticity in him. It modified both their attitudes about life.

"Did Darla tell you? She thinks she's learned the meaning of some of their words, at least in one of their languages. They seem to have more languages than there are stars," said Orwell. He smiled at Darla, obviously approving of her linguistic skills.

"What words did you learn, Darla?" Atom asked.

"Well, they don't name their planets like we did back home."

"Oh, you mean they don't name them by their orbital position?" asked Atom.

"That's right. Nor do they give them any numerical name."

"What do they call their planet?" asked Atom.

At that point, Evelyn rode up and joined them in the pilothouse, floating to her seat.

"We were just discussing the planet's name," said Atom.

"What is it called?" asked Evelyn.

"Earth. They call their planet, Earth," said Darla.

"Earth? That's an unusual name." Atom said it a few times to let it sink in and get the feel of it.

"And oddly enough, Earth sometimes is a synonym for dirt," continued Darla.

"Dirt?" said Orwell. "That's weird."

"Yes, it is," said Atom. They gave their planet a name which is not a scientific one. One that has nothing to distinctly quantify it, or describe its place in their planetary system."

"Indeed," reflected Evelyn. "Strange, when you think of it. However, **dirt** is <u>very</u> important to plants."

*   *   *

Later, they met in the recreation room. Since they arrived at the new planet, they had spent most of their time either gazing at Earth in the pilothouse, or watching the Earth's programs on TV that Orwell had tuned in. Evelyn still performed her greenhouse duties with as much commitment as before, but she did chores quicker so she could watch the TV. Especially since they planned to view the shows through the Verity Scanner.

"I don't know what we can expect," said Atom. "Obviously, the Scanner is not programmed with any of the Earth languages. Therefore, it may be a complete blank."

Atom and Orwell set up the Verity Scanner in the room facing the TV.

"The first part of the tripartite test, the V.I.P. or Verity Indicator Profile, can't have any effect because there isn't anything stored in the reputation file yet," said Orwell. "I wonder if it will work at all on this planet, considering the situation."

"I don't expect the third part of the test will work, either, unless Kronkite was brilliant enough to bypass the language problem. I guess what I'm trying to say is— not to expect miracles. All we have to go on is the second phase the test of truthfulness. The test of the speaker's voice, gestures, and facial irregularities— tics, duplicitous smiles, etc."

Orwell slouched comfortably on the couch with his arm around Darla. When Atom was finished, he sat down beside Evelyn.

The first picture on the screen was a woman in front of a map. She pointed to various symbols and made hand movements over some areas that the astronauts recognized, except for the symbols. They took note particularly of land shapes similar to the ones they had viewed telescopically.

"I saw the very cloud movement that she's pointing at," said Atom.

"I like her dress," said Darla. "Very stylish."

"The colors could be truer on the map, I think," said Evelyn. "It doesn't really show things as they appear from our vantage point. Land areas are cut into different color chunks."

"Maybe they just want to make it more colorful," said Darla snuggling

161

up to Orwell.

"The next picture showed a man talking behind a desk. There wasn't anything pictorial with the segment, so they couldn't understand what it was about.

No reaction came from the Verity Scanner.

Next, what appeared to be a game show came on. The host and contestants were very animated. Many luxury items were featured which Darla guessed were prizes. The Verity Scanner didn't respond to the show, except when the program's host was talking. It may have been an anomaly. Or, perhaps, the Scanner was responding to some insincerity on the part of the host. They were not sure.

After the game show, an action drama began. Immediately, the Verity Scanner responded. "It's working on this show," said Atom. "Maybe there's some hope for it after all." Back home, they knew that the Verity Scanner would be triggered by dramas. It was natural since actors were only pretending and delivering scripted lines that were fictional.

The story ended when the hero won and the villain was shot. Then followed a man who was, by his dress, pomp and display, some kind of dignitary. He had funny hair. He garnered much attention of those around him. Apparently, he was important. Behind him were all kinds of colorful banners. He spoke with great gusto to a very rapt adoring audience.

When he began to speak, the Verity Scanner reacted vigorously.

"That guy can't tell the truth, even when he's smiling," said Atom. "Look how pompous he is and how his chin juts out." They were all amused and amazed at the number of lies he told.

"I wonder what part of Earth that's coming from?" asked Evelyn.

"I don't know," answered Orwell. "It all depends on the planet's rotation and our satellite source."

"I wish Kronkite was here to see this," said Atom. "It proves his invention has cosmic utility."

Orwell beamed. "Honey, if we have a boy, let's name him Kronkite."

"That would have pleased Kronkite a lot, I know." said Atom, "And wouldn't he be happy to know that we've reached this beautiful living planet?"

"And also, that there is human life elsewhere in the universe," said Evelyn.

"You can say that again," added Orwell.

"Before we get too carried away, we've got lots to get ready. While we're all here together, it's a good time to discuss a few things. Orwell and I will have to pick a landing site. It must coincide with the planet's rotation and clear skies. That will require some weather forecasting on our part. Approaching the landing, we will have to slowly spiral in and still

162

maintain airspeed and not descend too rapidly and burn up in their atmosphere."

"So," finished Atom, "get the best sleep you can, for we'll need to be well-rested for what lies ahead of us."

The next day, they met in the recreation room again. It had become a regular time in their daily routine to share what they had learned about the Earth's inhabitants on television.

"I turned off the Verity Scanner," said Orwell. "There are so many liars making ridiculous claims, misrepresenting products, misleading their countrymen, fraudulently begging for donations— it became sickening. The weather reports are about all you can trust. From now on, I'm going to be more careful what I choose to watch."

Darla tried to soothe him. She knew how phony stuff annoyed him. "Don't let it get you down, honey."

"I won't. When you're aware of falsehood, you're partly safe." replied Orwell.

"Let's cheer up," said Evelyn. "We made a successful journey here. We found this beautiful planet. What more could we ask?"

"How's the language decoding coming, Darla?' asked Atom.

"I'm beginning to understand some of what they're saying, but not enough to carry on a conversation with any of them."

"Keep up your good work, Darla. We're definitely going to need your language facility when we come face to face with Earth's inhabitants. In the meantime, learn all you can about them."

"So, what's next, Atom? What have you determined we should do next?" asked Darla.

"Our flight in is not going to be an easy one. Orwell discovered we sustained some damage to our right rocket from the comet collision," said Atom.

"Why didn't you tell me?" asked Darla.

"I didn't want to worry you needlessly, honey," said Orwell.

"What about the damage?" Evelyn asked Atom.

"It means we must land on this planet. We couldn't continue interstellar travel, even if we wanted to, which I'm sure we don't want to anyway. Consider how fortunate we are to have finally discovered this habitable planet. Come, sweetheart, let's get some shuteye. Keep up your good work observing the Earthlings. Darla. Good night."

Much later that night, there came a loud knocking at their door. Atom and Evelyn woke quickly on hearing Darla's voice.

Atom jumped out of bed and opened the door. "Yes, what is it Darla?"

"Come down to the recreation room quickly. You've got to see this."

Evelyn and Atom threw on their robes and rushed to find Darla and

Orwell glued to the television set.

"What's going on?"

"We're the major topic of all the news channels on Earth," said Darla. "Apparently, an amateur astronomer, while stargazing, discovered Starfarer's orbit and reported it. We're being watched by everyone all over the world. The people are panicking. Some fear we're an invader from outer space. Others fear that we're a secret weapon of one of their neighbors and expect to be attacked. Leaders are in a frenzy. Armed forces are being called up and they're manning their rocket defense sites."

"Folks, we have a problem," said Atom.

CHAPTER XXXV

Always on Atom's mind was the task facing him, landing Starfarer. It weighed heavily on him. He agonized over piloting the spaceship to a safe landing. Except for training on the flight simulator, he had never experienced landing such a large craft, nor had anyone else. He would be the first. Orwell would, of course, assist him. Whatever decisions were to be made, however, would all be Atom's. He would be solely in charge. Was he good enough? Had he studied enough? Was he overlooking any important factors he should attend to? The responsibility sometimes overwhelmed him.

The Starfarer astronauts had risked everything to search the cosmos for a new livable planet. Did life exist in other galaxies? It was the unanswered question that had vexed astronomers for centuries. Should their home planet be destroyed as some predicted, only migration could preserve their species. For this cause, Atom, Evelyn, Darla, and Orwell had made the commitment. They had volunteered for Kronkite's space project. It had taken years of their lives. Now on the verge of success would it all come to naught?

This was the question. Of course, Kronkite and the people back home would never know whether Starfarer's flight succeeded or not, unless a superior form of communication could be developed to radio the news back to them from such a vast distance. However, the inhabitants of this new planet, Earth, would learn that life existed elsewhere. It would be extremely valuable information for the Earthlings.

In all of history, it's not out of the ordinary for explorers never to return or never be heard from again. Some are lost at sea, some are lost in unexplored wildernesses, and some are attacked and killed by natives of the territory visited.

What was to be the fate of the Starfarer group?

"Darla and Orwell, you've studied the Earthling's activities the most. What is your idea on the situation?" asked Atom. "What have you learned from their television shows? Bring me up to date."

"We've monitored various locations," reported Darla. "The news programs all seem to suggest a flurry of war preparation."

"Yes," agreed Orwell, "the Earthlings seem to be very violent. The planet is plagued with wars. It's even common to have killings, massacres, and bombings daily in the news. The Verity Scanner has revealed that they are easily misled by some tyrants who teach and preach fear and hatred. They are entirely dogma-driven starting from childhood."

"How can we convince them that we come in peace?"

"That's a good question, Evelyn," said Darla.

"I've given that question a lot of thought, too. I believe through radio we could transmit them a message."

"That's a good idea, Orwell," said Atom brightening at the suggestion.

"Yes, I've thought of that idea, too," countered Darla. "The problem is I'm not fluent enough in any of their thousands of languages, to do it."

Like every good solution that lacks means, the idea withered on the vine. Then Evelyn brainstormed an alternative she thought might be beneficial.

"Why don't we broadcast some of Atom's music, especially some of his most happy and melodious songs. It's often said that music soothes the savage beast. It's also said that music is the universal language."

"Sweetheart, that's a good idea. Maybe it will show that we're peace-loving and our intentions are good. Now aren't you glad I included my music collection in our baggage allowance?"

"I like the idea," said Darla. I'll start right away. I'll be the first disc jockey to the stars."

The dark cloud of their situation still lingered, but for the moment their spirits were lifted.

*   *   *

Days of orbiting, observing, and planning passed. They made copious notes of the Earthling's activities as seen on television. They tried to assess what kind of reception they could expect if they attempted to land Starfarer on Earth. The rocket defense silos were viewed as particularly ominous.

Darla as DJ was doing a good job. One of Atom's songs was rebroadcast on Earth's news shows. It was gratifying to see some of the Earthlings smiling and looking less fearful. Yet a lot of suspicion remained.

Crowds were shown gathering and protesting that not enough was being done to protect the citizenry from foreign invasion. People were stocking shelters for their own safety. Many were buying guns to protect themselves from space invaders. Some group leaders were whipping up their fearful followers into a frenzy. Focusing on the spaceship as an enemy enhanced the influence of rabble-rousing demagogues.

Some of the more militant leaders advocated a preemptive strike against the alien spaceship. Better safe than sorry. Shoot first, sort it out after.

Conspiracy theorists were quick to come up with their own fanciful opinions.

Some were even convinced that it was a sign that Judgment Day had come as punishment for sinners. Other gloomy prophets suggested it might be a signal of divine retribution like plagues and floods. Space people? Anyone not of their group was not to be trusted, regardless.

As usual, after dining, the astronauts convened to discuss their situation and make plans. So far, Atom had kept a wide orbit course around the earth. They were still very grateful they had found a planet in the whole of the cosmos which was livable and had beings on it similar to themselves. They could hardly believe their good fortune about that. Nevertheless, a lot of uncertainty remained.

Then Darla began to notice a change in Orwell. As days passed, he was growing more restless. He was indeed impulsive, but were his impulses correct? That was the question. What bothered him?

"Are we just going to go 'round and 'round in circles the rest of our lives? All the while, with a paradise awaiting us? All we have to do is get our feet on the ground," said Orwell.

Atom understood Orwell's irritation. He also felt the weight of complications he faced in landing Starfarer on the planet. "Patience never hurt," he said.

"You're too Kronkite cautious, that's your problem," growled Orwell.

Evelyn and Darla cringed at the growing confrontation.

"Maybe," said Darla, "the Earthlings will forget us— that our novelty will wear off."

"We can't just sail around forever hoping they'll forget us," said Orwell becoming more agitated. "I'll tell you another thing which I haven't wanted to worry you about."

Orwell paused, while the wives became attentive.

"Since our asteroid collision, our propulsion rockets are not all in good condition. It may come to a point where we have no choice, either land, or burn up in their atmosphere."

"Is that true?" Evelyn asked Atom.

He nodded ruefully, yes.

It became more silent than silence. Each astronaut retreated into a private meditative mode.

"That settles it!" Orwell stood up abruptly. "We've just been floating around in limbo. I say you lack the courage to go in for a landing. Accept it. There is no more that we can do except make a decision and act on it. We can't keep putting it off. Isn't that true? Do we have to test you with the Verity Scanner?"

"Okay, okay." said Atom. We're still operational. But you're right, time is against us. I've picked a potential landing site which I have charted. Here it is. Look it over for yourselves. I want your opinions. I won't do anything we don't all agree on."

There was a long silence with heads bowed in quiet thought. Orwell reached over and placed his hand in Darla's and looked searchingly into her eyes. It was a communication that only spouses share. It had been a long journey. They had endured much. Darla's child was growing within her. In silence, they gazed at one another searching for consensus. All knew the risk they were taking. The decision had to be made, and it had to be unanimous.

"All right. Let's take a vote," said Orwell. "We've made our preparations, I say we go for it tomorrow. Darla, how do you vote?"

Darla nodded a solemn yes.

"So, it's up to you two," said Orwell.

Evelyn turned towards Atom. The seriousness of the decision swept over her. It could be a grand new beginning or a tragic end. She tried to read Atom's feelings because so much of the burden was on him.

"What is your vote, Evelyn?" asked Orwell.

Evelyn and Atom stood face to face. They held hands.

Atom looked in her eyes and made a gentle nod. "Our answer is... yes."

The four astronauts agreed. After all the years of space travel confined in Starfarer, the decision was made, they would go in for a landing if possible... tomorrow!

<u>CHAPTER XXXVI</u>

Tomorrow, and tomorrow, and tomorrow, came and went. All the while, Starfarer orbited, like a moon, slowly around and around the Earth, the planet which the astronauts yearned to call home.

They all had many concerns about the planet. It was the subject of much table talk. How would they be received by the planet's occupants? Would they confront nasty, brutish, superstitious savages? Or would they find exceptional, enlightened, civil individuals? Would they be met with weapons or welcome?

Would the planet's societies be coercive and corrupt, or generous and compassionate?

What stage of evolution were they in? Were the citizens intelligent or irrational? Free or subservient?

So many questions. So few answers.

Foremost was landing. Would they be able to land safely?

"If we orbit one more time, I'll go mad!" declared Orwell. He was impatient with Atom because he kept putting off the landing.

"We have to choose our landing spot very carefully." Atom said, examining surface photos. "We don't know the terrain. We need a long runway. the longest we can find."

Starfarer was well-designed. It had taken them safely through interstellar travel. The journey had taken years. Everything was converging on this, the culmination of it all. The expedition's summit. The crucial, never before attempted, landing! Its outcome was dangerously uncertain.

Anyone who enters a strange new place has experienced the trepidation of the unfamiliar, be it a first day at school, a new job, moving to a new community. The step the astronauts were taking was more hazardous than any of those; more fraught with danger.

As a skydiver must feel a moment of hesitation before he jumps, so the Starfarer astronauts were poised on the brink of this momentous irreversible leap of faith. Landing Starfarer!

Orwell felt the urgency keenly. One reason was Starfarer's damaged rocket. The second was more personal— Darla was expecting. He had maintained the spacecraft in flight as well as he could. It was almost as if the rocket's workings were a living part of his biological being. Since launch, however, both had aged. How reliable were Starfarer's controls now?

The astronauts continued to work, despite the delay. For years, they had performed their jobs routinely in the narrow confines of the rocket ship. The life they lived aboard was practically like being in a prison. It was a prison without guards. No guards were needed. They were held captive, walled in by SPACE.

Darla dutifully attempted to make radio contact. She had tried to master one of Earth's languages. She hoped to inform the Earthlings of Starfarer's peaceful intentions, and thus, pave the way for their arrival. With the exception of Atom's music, as far as they knew, no other contact was made. What attitude the people of Earth held for them, they didn't know. They continued to monitor broadcasts from satellites, learning all that they could from what they saw visually on Earth television.

Evelyn continued her horticultural tasks. Plants were her life. Preservation of the plants preserved their lives. It was a job she couldn't very well retire from. She took special care preparing the plants for landing. Some of her hybrids might adapt to the new environment, she thought. The plants might prove to be valuable new species for the planet Earth.

Atom felt the ultimate responsibility. He had found a worthy destination. The question was, could he land Starfarer safely?

They gathered for a regular meeting in their dining area to further discuss the situation. Orwell was the first to speak.

"Atom, I understand your hesitation about landing. I really do. But— forgive me for being blunt— Darla and I feel you've taken every precaution, and...what I mean to say is...we're ready. Nothing can guarantee a successful landing. We know that. We're lucky to have found a habitable planet. Life is all chance and Darla and I are ready to take that chance."

A few seconds of silence followed. Evelyn tried to read her husband's face while he pondered his reply. So much was riding on this final crucial step.

"Is it the landing, or what we'll face on landing?" asked Orwell. "I know the mindset of some of the planet's inhabitants is strange. Like, why they have so many wars, and what causes them. Whatever the reason— tyrannical leaders, ignorant followers, or both— it's hard to comprehend why they choose warfare over the welfare of their citizens. But we've come this far, whatever is to be, we've got to take the risk. That, or live out our lives endlessly drifting in the nowhere of space."

"Back home, we did have a lot of the negatives Orwell mentions," said Darla.

"Yes," said Atom, "we did have many, that is, until Kronkite's invention."

"That's true, until the Verity Scanner exposed the *myth-informed*," quipped Orwell, repeating Kronkite's old joke. "And, I might add, the Verity Scanner did away with **fake** *myth-management*, as well. And I'm *not* lisping when I say that."

They all had a stress-relieving laugh at Orwell's revision of Kronkite's old gag.

"One thing let's never forget, no matter what happens," said Evelyn, joining hands with Atom, Darla, and Orwell, "let's never lose our love of each other or… our love of freedom."

Atom smiled at his wife. "Well put. I think, that says it all. We're ready to land. We don't know much about this planet, or its inhabitants. Are they free or oppressed? Enlightened or superstitious? The one thing we do know is, we have something of value to offer them— something that assures honesty and integrity— the Verity Scanner!"

                          *   *   *

Finally, after another busy day of preparations, the astronauts again convened in the dining room. Their spirits were elevated. After enduring years of interstellar space travel, the end was in sight, the dream was to be fulfilled, a new home!

"Well folks, this should be our last supper in space," said Atom.

The announcement was expected, yet somehow sounded unexpected. Some things we know are coming, when they come, they still surprise us.

"At last! I couldn't have taken one more day of orbiting," said Orwell.

Evelyn and Darla looked at each other and offered hesitant smiles. It was all so final.

"All gear stashed? Suits at the ready? I think we are as prepared as we can get. Any questions?" Atom paused. He looked steadfastly at each of his Starfarer mates. While remaining silent, all recognized the seriousness of the announcement.

"Okay, get a good night's sleep. Ride up "the can" to the pilothouse at six tomorrow morning. Then, suit up, and be prepared for the big day. Our grand entrance. A new beginning."

Their excitement was intense. It was like the night before the launch. Like facing an important exam. They did indeed face a test. Sleeping was not easy. It was a restless night for them all.

                          *   *   *

Exactly at six the next day, the astronauts met in the pilothouse. All outfitted in their space suits, they occupied the seats that years before they sat in for launching. It was a somber group. Even Orwell was not his usual jocular self.

"Thank you for being on time," said Atom. "Before we leave this orbit, I want to thank you for your cooperation. We couldn't have existed without it. I sometimes doubted myself, but I never felt you doubted me, and for that I thank you. Now, buckle up everybody."

"Darla, be careful with your belt restraints," said Orwell. "Evelyn, give her a hand, will you?"

Atom waited till they all acknowledged they were ready. Then, Atom switched off the autopilot and took control of Starfarer.

"Ready, Orwell? Step number one. Apply the brakes on the artificial gravity cylinder."

"Aye, aye, Captain," Orwell said with his usual stress-relieving humor, before beginning the procedure. A noise, unusual to their ears, was heard. It was followed by a vibration-like trembling, that all felt in the pilothouse. Atom tightly gripped the controls, as their former living quarters slowed and ceased spinning.

"Anti-gravity rotation step completed," Orwell announced.

"Step two. We're going to start spiraling in. Orwell, watch the radar. We don't want to smash any of their satellites if we can help it. That would be an unfriendly act. Darla, keep track of any radio contacts that you receive. If you get any contacts that are meaningful to you, let me know. We all have to keep focused as we circle and close in on the planet."

The little azure blue dot of a planet was in sight, and was gradually increasing to a size much larger than before. Features were becoming more visible than they had been telescopically. The similarity to their own home planet was striking and reassuring. It was thrilling to behold.

"I'll be looking for a long salt flat that appears geographically vacant with sufficient runway length for us. We certainly want to avoid any heavily populated areas."

As Starfarer plummeted towards Earth, features began to increase in size and detail. Oceans and geological terrain were visible first, and then rivers, roads, buildings....

"The surface appears to be about two-thirds water," judged Orwell. "I don't think we want to land in the soup."

"The water is fine, but look at the greenery," said Evelyn marveling at the sight.

"Atom, we're receiving radar hits!"

"It'll be all right, Darla, if the hits are not acted upon."

In many of the passes, they encountered the planet's moon. As they circled in farther, where the planet was shaded from the rays of the sun, the illumination they had distantly seen was now clearly evident. It was the artificial lighting of towns and cities.

"Wouldn't Kronkite have been thrilled to see this," said Darla, "a habitable planet, one that he could only have dreamed existed."

"And think how Sara would have loved to study the formation and evolution of their societies," said Evelyn. "How they live and interact with each other."

More features became visible as their rocket decelerated. It became an on-and-off blinking light show. When they rounded to the day surface of the planet, Evelyn exclaimed, "Look at the patches. Those are evidence of agriculture. I'm sure of it."

Now more of the planet filled their vision. As the planet spun below them, it filled more and more of their viewing window.

"The gauges show our exterior is heating up. So far, we haven't reached a dangerous level. Heat shields, don't fail us," said Orwell, his eyes glued to the temperature readings. "Hello, gravity. Hello, atmosphere. Hello, air."

Now the terrain and physical geography was clearly defined.

"Although the continental shapes are different," said Orwell excitedly, "I almost feel like I'm returning home."

Atom, sweating profusely, had a tight grip on the controls. "Prepare to retrofire rockets," he commanded.

Evelyn, smiling at Darla, became very reflective. "We were plucked up by our roots, but here we'll grow and thrive. I feel it."

Darla quipped in return, "Wouldn't Sara have had a psychological field day, studying the Earthlings."

The land streamed by them in a blur of motion.

"Prepare to activate landing gear," commanded Atom.

"Landing gear ready, Atom."

"Rockets all set for retrofire, Orwell?"

"Set, you bet."

"Okay. Landing gear down?"

"Landing gear down!" yelled Orwell, as the land's surface sped by under them.

"Be prepared to deploy the chutes and set the brakes! The salt flat I'm looking for is just beyond that mountain range. Keep an eye out for it!"

"I see the flat, Atom!" shouted Evelyn.

"Retrofire rockets and hit the brakes, Orwell!"

Out of Starfarer, came a surging rush, roar, and rumble!

"Hold on, everybody!" Atom called out. "It's gonna be a rough landing...!"

THE END

173

About the Author

The first favorable response **Edward McClenathan** received for some of his early writings was from Nobel Prize winner, Bertrand Russell. The writings are archived among Bertrand Russell's files at McMaster University, Hamilton, Canada.

Many projects were to follow. He and his sons wrote a musical comedy called "**Oh, Hennery!**" Printed versions (play & musical) will soon be available. During a run of the musical in Jamestown, New York, the author was involved in a Dramatist Guild seminar with Stephen Sondheim, Arthur Miller, Jules Feiffer, and other notable writers.

Besides the above, Ed has won numerous writing contests. The most recent was a small contest held by the Chautauqua Book Club (CLSC). Entrants were to select a line from a speech delivered in the Chautauqua Amphitheater and form a couplet. For the contest, he selected a line from comedian Lewis Black. The entry was:

> *No one should live this long* (Lewis Black)
> *Devoid of love, laughter, and song.* (Edward McClenathan)

Edward McClenathan studied art at Carnegie Mellon and holds several degrees in Speech, Education, Library Science, and English from the State University of New York at Fredonia and the University of Buffalo. He is a member of the Bertrand Russell and Charles Dickens Societies.

Other Edacious Reader Books™ include:

"Cat vs. Dog"
(available at Amazon.com)

"Holidays and Hoopla"
(available at Amazon.com)

ATO ["Adjusted Traditional Orthography"] A phonetic-learning-to-read and spell alphabet.

Made in the USA
Columbia, SC
28 July 2020